LUCKEY K.D.

Living With My Superpowers

First edition

ISBN: 979-8-9910319-5-0

This book was professionally typeset on Reedsy.
Find out more at reedsy.com

To my incredible family, whose unwavering support and love have been my greatest superpowers.

To my children, for inspiring me with your boundless imagination and reminding me that heroes come in all shapes and sizes.

My friends have always believed in me, even when I doubted myself.

And to every reader, may you find the courage to embrace your own unique powers and the strength to face your inner battles. This book is for you.

Contents

ABDUCTED

It would have been a night to be grateful for the lights the street provided as Dr. Fowler scuttled along. But only two or three of them worked at this time. The grey sky overhead had only made plans for a normal night and so had locked the moon away.

A thousand and one eyes pierced through the dark, watching every move he made. Someone was on his trail. He could feel the zephyr of wind that gave their stealth away. He strained his searching eyes through the darker shades cast by the fir and sycamore trees. Yet the stalker remained elusive.

With his suit flapping and briefcase dangling like it was suspended by a spring, his thick legs paddled his bulky frame. The ground swayed beneath his feet. It took extra effort to keep his knees from buckling even as anxiety clutched at them.

He halted suddenly. A pair of bulging hazel eyes scanned the surroundings. He had just felt that gust of wind whoosh past him again – much closer this time.

"Who's there?" he called out.

The speech was almost impossible. It felt as though he had a shard of glass in his throat. And loosening his tie didn't make it any better, although his Adam's apple seemed to bob much easier as he swallowed hard.

His call met with an unforgiving silence. Peace apparently hung in the air. But it was the type that threatened his safety. With his muscles agitating for freedom, there was one thing he could do at this point: RUN! But not with legs that were as heavy as a boulder. They were meant to carry his bulk, not flip him through a distance.

Propelled by what was left of his courage, he moved further, hoping it was all a mirage, hoping he was only being paranoid.

But hardly had he taken a step when a thought waltzed into his mind.

He took out his phone and tapped on it, but the lights didn't come on. He tapped again and again, but the phone stayed dark.

"SHIT!" he spat.

He looked up again. It was unnerving that a thousand eyes bore down on him, yet he saw no one. He could feel them hanging on the treetops and behind the trunks.

He stood in the brightness of the street lamp. He felt a bit safer here. He could see everything around him, and it was much easier to spot the stalker. He thought to stay on the spot for a moment until someone found him. The grayness beyond this spot held a sense of foreboding.

But he couldn't possibly pass the night under a lamppost. He looked down the gray street that appeared darker in the lights. The thought of going through it got his heart skipping beats.

He sized up the surroundings once again. And with his fingers curled tight around the handle of his briefcase, he trudged on.

His eyes shot in every direction as he advanced deeper into the gray night. Fear clawed at his heart, smashing it against the walls of his chest. His grip around the briefcase' handle only got tighter.

Suddenly, a black minivan whizzed forward and pulled over right in front of him, its tires screeching. The absence of headlights meant it had come from somewhere close.

The door rolled aside. Two men stormed out. Dressed in thick black jackets and faces half-hidden in baseball caps, they looked like men of special ops. One of them had his hands on an Armalite AR-10A2 - the other leveled what looked like a custom-made Desert Eagle at Dr. Fowler – both hands hidden in thick black gloves.

Dr. Fowler put his hands in the air – his briefcase hanging down his right hand. As the man with the pistol stormed toward him, he stepped backward. Adrenaline pumped through his veins for an immediate response.

But one more step and his body thudded lightly against a wall behind. He jerked and turned back. A man dressed like the two others before him stood like a column in a temple. Dr. Fowler could feel his mouth warm as he swallowed a lump of saliva. It was the stalker! For one thing, he deserved a punch for all the heartache he made him go through.

Instead, he pushed the doctor toward the man coming for him. Dr. Fowler kept his hands in the air as the men chauffeured him toward the car. A mist of sweat trailed his forehead, even as shivers coursed down his spine.

Just as he was about to step into the car, he heard a voice from behind:

"Let him go!"

Everyone looked back. A lady was walking toward them in long, calculated strides. Her brown leather pants and jacket made her look like a decorated assassin. It was hard to escape that thought, not with her hair tied in a ponytail – eyes and nose hidden in a mask.

"And if we don't let him go?" the man with the Armalite spoke, stepping forward - hands firm on the rifle.

The lady stood a few feet away and did not say another word.

"It was pretty easy to lure you out, Azra," intoned the one with the pistol. We knew you would come to save the day…" he glanced skyward, "or, I should say, the night."

Azra tilted her head backward and closed her eyes. She spread her arms wide apart. And as if pulling on some invisible pillars, she forced her arms closer.

The first guy cocked his rifle. "But you've fucking come to the end of the road…"

He opened fire on Azra. A crackle of gunshots split the air like fireworks, launching a barrage of bullets like a meteor shower. But a wall of water stood before Azra like an elastic shield. Denser than oil, it acted like some impenetrable force. The bullets tore halfway through it and bounced off.

The men were not deterred. They pumped more bullets at her, hoping to break through the wall. But some of them got lost in it – the rest clatter on the ground. Azra had her arms stretched forward, keeping the force on the wall.

Having exhausted the bullets in their magazines, the men ceased fire, and the street once again observed a moment of silence.

Azra dropped her hands, releasing the force on the water. As it splattered on the ground, the bullets it had swallowed clinked like nails on a marble floor.

"You think you're tough, huh? Do you think your superpowers can save you? Well, you got something else coming…"

He dug into a pouch on his jacket and took out another magazine. As they both reloaded, Azra strode toward them, almost as swift as a bullet.

She took hold of the rifle as he was about to push the magazine in position. He raised his head and threw a punch at her. She ducked. At the same time, she kicked off the pistol in the other man's hand. It clattered on the ground a few feet away. The first guy pulled on his gun to snatch it back, but she gave him a headbutt on the nose.

While the man with the pistol engaged her in a fight, the stalker pushed Dr. Fowler into the bus. He seemed to have realized his men had slim chances of winning the fight.

Azra hurled what looked like darts at the tires before her, deflating them. The driver probably noticed for he yelled:

"COME ON, GUYS, LET'S GET OUTTA HERE."

But his men were locked in a fight with Azra and couldn't get away. The second man heard the call and made for the car. But Azra pulled him on his jacket and delivered a punch so powerful it had him reeling sideways. In a swift movement of the leg, she fired a kick at the other man. He lolloped toward the car. Azra moved forward to pull him back, but his colleague cut her off.

He threw punches at her. One by one, she blocked them off easily. Her defense was faster, her movements swift. The man flung his foot toward her face. She grabbed it and bunged it aside. As he staggered forward, she kicked him on his scapula, her wedge heel almost tearing through his flesh. He yelled and fell to the ground.

Azra went for him at once. But the stalker shot at her from the car. She swayed from side to side in quick, successive steps, dodging the bullets.

"COME ON, MAN!"

The distraction allowed the man the chance to dive into the vehicle. At once, it zoomed off, grinding the tires against the tarmac.

As soon as they drove away, Azra dropped on her knee. Her face crumpled with a sharp wince. She placed her hand on her side and then raised it to her face. Blood! She wasn't fast enough.

"You're hurt!" a voice spoke.

Azra looked up and quickly got on her feet in a gallant attempt to hide her pain. Before her was a girl she surmised could be in her mid-20s. Her black biker jacket and leather pants suggested she could also be a fighter like her. But immediately, Azra stood up; she raised her hands submissively.

"I can take you to the hospital if you want," she added, walking toward her.

Azra stared suspiciously at her, barely hiding the questions in her eyes. "Who are you?"

"My name is Zuri. I'm a fan. I've been following your operations for a while now…"

"You've been spying on me?" Azra's brows crinkled.

"No, not at all. I'm not a spy. I want to be a part of your team."

"That's not possible, kid. Go home!" She herself turned and limped toward the exit.

But Zuri caught up with her. "I'm not a kid. I'm 24. And I can fight. I'm pretty techy, too. I want to join you, please."

Azra did not reply but kept walking.

"I know your true identity…"

Azra stopped in her tracks and looked at her. Her brows creased lightly.

"I've seen you a number of times return to your house and remove the mask. I also know your real name is Jasmine."

Azra took an intimidating step toward her - a frown darkening her features.

"I'm sorry I invaded your privacy." Zuri backed away swiftly. "I just wanted to be a part of something real, something meaningful."

Azra stopped, her hand applying pressure on her wound. Again, she stared at Zuri. Perhaps this time, she saw the honesty in her words, the burning desire to be a part of her team.

"Go home!" she warned.

That was disappointing! Zuri thought she had struck the right nerve when she stopped.

But now she turned and limped away, pressing against her ribs. Zuri merely gazed at her as she dissolved into the dark.

OLD GLEN C

lood slurped as Jasmine guided a pair of forceps through her skin. She'd turned purple in the face. Tiny veins threatened to pop beneath her skin. But even as pangs of pain seared through her body, she did not stop probing her entrails. It was not her first time – not her first time removing a bullet from her own body. Being 'Azra' means being a rugged individualist.

Luckily, the bullet had only penetrated shallowly. It was easier to find. Jasmine sucked air through clenched teeth as she clipped the bullet and gently pulled it out.

She gasped as the cone-shaped killer left her body, covered in blood and tissue. Her eyes were still shut as she took in the pain. The hand holding the bullet shuddered like it was freezing.

She quickly stuffed a wad of cotton wool on the spot and wrapped strips of bandages around it.

A light knock came on the door. "Honey, are you in there?"

She hurriedly gathered her tools and dropped them in the cabinet next to her bed. Taking a quick look around to be sure nothing suspicious was left in the open, she pulled down her shirt to cover the bandage.

"Yes, honey. Come on in," she answered, repressing the pain in her voice.

She adjusted her bottom on the bed and titivated her hair. At the same time, the door creaked inward. Her husband came through.

"Darling, are you all right?" he crooned, moving to the bed.

"I'm fine, honey. Just coming in?" She had judged from the shirt and trousers he was putting on.

His brows drew together as he sniffed in hard. "What's that smell?"

"What smell?" Jasmine's eyes darted. Of course, she knew what he was talking about.

He exhaled sharply and waved his hand. "Don't bother about that. I arrived 30 minutes ago. I couldn't find you anywhere in the house."

Jasmine heaved a breath, trying to keep a cheerful countenance. "I stepped out to get some fresh air. The kids are giving me a hard time…" she giggled.

He slid his hand across her neck to cheer her up, fingers hidden behind her hair. "Are you sure you're okay, honey?"

She nodded. "Why?"

Her eyes shifted to the corners. Her own body betrayed her. Although she knew it would be difficult to hide her body language from a medical scientist.

"You're running a temperature," he observed

"I'm fine. I guess it's the temperature in the room…"

But Michael didn't think that was the reason. He recoiled to examine her closely. But she snapped off quickly and got on her feet.

"Did you check on the kids?"

"Yes. They're sleeping."

She flung her hair to the back and began to tie it in a ponytail. "Did you get the result you've been working for?"

Micheal breathed a deep breath and got on his feet. "Nah, not yet, still working on it…"

* * *

Because of Michael's intrusion, Jasmine did not get enough time to patch herself up properly. But while he snored, she had loosened the bandages and treated the wound.

She worked from home as a digital marketer. Most times, Michael took the kids to school. And either they returned on the school bus, or she would go and get them in her car.

It was the regular routine this morning. Michael had kissed her on the cheeks.

"Bye, mommy," Audrey and Melissa had bid.

Jasmine stood by the door, smiling and waving at them as Michael shut it.

And now, she was seated at her dressing table. The light from her computer reflected on her face. She had deflated the tires last night and planted a tracker on the car. The darts were merely a distraction.

She rolled the mouse around a spot while clicking on it. Her eyes moved with the same precision. Having confirmed her password, she landed on the locator domain. The tracker had been programmed for easy access. But this time, a glitch had it presenting unusual data.

The domain was blank, even with a strong signal. It seemed like the tracker had been discovered and squashed underfoot. But Jasmine was certain that was not the case. It would be impossible to open the domain if it was.

The mouse clicked as she repeatedly tapped her finger on it, rolling it around the desk. Her eyes settled on the screen, unblinking. With steady breathing, she hoped it would come on soon. And it did!

The screen turned from gray to lemon. A map gradually spread out on the screen like a blanket. Ripples of red light flashed from a location pin somewhere on the map. Jasmine wasted no time clicking on it.

The spot zoomed in at once, carrying a location tag that read: 'Old Glen C warehouse'. This was somewhere along 442 Road, east of River Canali.

"Gotcha!" Jasmine exclaimed.

She took note of the coordinates and the marks within the perimeter.

After getting the details she needed, she stared at the location pin and everything around it. Memories of the man being held hostage at the spot flashed in her head like bolts of lightning.

Dr. Fowler might be a bad man himself - her relationship with him may not have ended well, but he didn't deserve to be kept as a hostage. No one knew about her secret identity, so it couldn't have been the reason he was kidnapped.

Jasmine's eyes darted to the top corner of the screen, and a light frown etched up on her face. What about the girl...? Zuri? Could she have hired those guys? Her brows twisted.

But the tension on her face soon began to lighten up. Zuri didn't seem like she could do something like that, yet show up to her face, claiming to be a fan and wanting to join her crusade.

* * *

Day had succumbed to the silence of the night. Except for crickets buzzing faintly in the distance, one would have heard the sound of a pin dropping a few meters away. The curtains were drawn, the lights were out, and the streets were cold. But not so cold for Azra.

She had levitated out of her house through a square opening on her roof. Her husband and kids were fast asleep, and she was just a lady working an extra shift.

She pushed a Kawasaki Ninja ZX-14R out to the street—a mobile means buried in a basement behind her house. Her husband, Michael, had no idea he had a basement sitting somewhere in the foundation of his property. And she was not ready to divulge that—maybe not yet.

She mounted on the bike and took up her helmet.

"You will need help out there," intoned that voice again.

It traveled with the wind, loud and clear. Azra looked across the road. Zuri emerged from the dark, dressed for the occasion.

"Stalking me will do you no good," Azra replied, settling the helmet on her head.

Zuri clicked her tongue. "Trust me: I'm not enjoying it either. But…"

"I don't need help." Azra slots the key through the hole. "And if I catch you stalking me again, I will not be held responsible for whatever happens to you."

She turned on the ignition and revved the bike. It growled like a bear. She hit the gear and zoomed off - not a glance at the loyal soldier standing by her.

Zuri was stranded and abandoned just like before. But this time, throwing herself in the line of fire seemed like her only choice.

* * *

6 minutes to Old Glen C. Azra navigated the streets and highways. The Kawasaki Ninja, streamlined for speed, cut through the wind. With a firm grip on the handle, Azra fired on, swaying past cars as though they were at a standstill.

Saving Dr. Fowler was a top priority. But perhaps if she gave it a second thought, she would realize she could be walking into a trap. She could be the target, after all.

The bike leaned inward as it rounded a traffic circle like in MotoGP. Azra's hair flew in the drought, making her resemble a model on a photo shoot. Car horns blared ceremoniously as she zipped past them, leaving behind a chain of collisions. 6 minutes seemed like a short time, but too long for her.

She rode through an alleyway and stormed out to the next street. The bike growled as she turned toward a narrow path between a stretch of lawn. The tires screeched to a halt at a point. The path was closed. She couldn't tear through the gate. It wasn't worth it. She stared at it while her mind worked on which way to follow – the bike revving all the while.

A screech of the tires had her sliding back down the path. She soon stormed out of the street, off another road that led her to 442 Road.

Her hair flailed with the wind as she accelerated at more than 50 miles per hour. She veered through an even shorter route, which finally brought her to Old Glen C.

It was the size of a lawn tennis court and just as high. Azra parked behind a truck several meters away from the building. Standing by it, she observed the surroundings. She couldn't find the car she had bugged anywhere, just the bike parked in front of the warehouse. It was dark and quiet as if there was no one behind those closed doors. Mist from the River Canal made her nose flare, filling up her lungs and refreshing her muscles. The willow trees on the other side of the building would serve as cover for her when things got ugly, she thought.

She pulled the Smith and Wesson Model 3566 pistol from its holster strapped to her waist. She cocked it - eyes on the warehouse.

In the cover of darkness, she crept toward the building - limbs swift. Her senses were on sharp alert. Her fingers curled tight around the handle, with her index just in front of the trigger and ready to pull.

As stealthy as a lioness on a hunt, she arrived at one of the windows. She opened it through a few centimeters and looked through. She couldn't see the ends of the warehouse, but she saw Dr. Fowler tied to a chair – lips sealed shut with duct tape. The stalker stood by him like a bodyguard, bearing a gun in his hand. The warehouse itself was studded with cartons stacked high in rows.

Azra stretched further to examine the door area. But her head pushed the window, and it creaked. She quickly pulled back.

Now, she crept toward the door, making sure her boots didn't crunch hard against the pebbles. The wind whooshed across her face, flailing her hair but not exaggerating her presence. Her footsteps were precise and calculated. There was no window closer to the door – she would have looked through.

She glanced at the bike. She thought it was no match for hers in a race. And having sized up the surroundings once again, she wrapped her fingers gently on the door's handle. Her other hand had the gun in a cautious grip.

She opened the door 3 cm and pushed it further. Her head peeked through, but she could only see Dr. Fowler, who appeared asleep. The stalker was not with him.

With her body's swift, decisive movement, she filtered through the door and hid behind a stack of cartons. She feared the stalker might have noticed her presence and taken cover.

She surveyed the warehouse. The stale smell of paper filled the air. Bags and ropes piled high on the left side of the door. With the cartons stacked in rows, it would be easier to meander her way out.

Her head peeked out from its hiding place. She observed the stalker had returned. He didn't notice her presence after all. It also occurred to her that the cartons behind him were more closely packed. It was difficult to see what or who was behind them.

Azra withdrew her head and stared vacantly for a moment.

Quick decision!

She exhaled through her pouted lips and peeped again. The stalker was still standing by Dr. Fowler.

She crept behind the row, scanning every corner for the other members. Fits of shuffling came from behind the cartons. She stopped, gazing apprehensively at the area. The other members were there. Now, she must take care of the stalker discreetly.

She walked as if fragile glass, one step at a time. One wrong move, and she would have the cartons crashing down, revealing her presence.

She got close enough. The stalker was on the side of the row. The cartons blocked off the zephyr of wind that might have given away her location.

She poked her head out. The stalker had his eyes on the entrance.

With a burst of speed and agility, Azra stormed out of her lair and struck the stalker's neck with her gun. He faded and thudded on the ground at once. The noise might have alerted the others, Azra feared. Just as it did Dr. Fowler.

He opened his eyes and winced, and his features swam. He looked wasted and in desperate need of rest. It was all blurry at first, and the yellow lights overhead made it even worse. Azra yanked the tape off his mouth. He hummed and shook his head in pain.

As his eyes got acquainted with the environment, they soon fell on the lady trying to cut him loose.

"Who… are you?"

His voice defined weakness and hopelessness.

But Azra shushed him, making the sibilant sign of whispering. She cut off the ropes and took his hand. Dr. Fowler growled lightly as she helped him to his feet.

With his hand across her shoulders, she led him toward the door. The stalker remained unconscious all the while.

But upon reaching the door, Azra looked back. She saw him tilt back to life. Time to hurry up.

The door creaked. And that brought the stalker fully alert. Azra and Dr. Fowler had just made it through when he fired shots at them. The bullets tore through the architrave, barely missing the targets.

The stalker scrambled to his feet and went after them. The shot ignited the other members' fight response. About four of them stormed out from behind the cartons.

Just as the stalker dashed out of the entrance, bullets splattered on the door and architrave. He fell back in, lucky not to have been hit.

Azra had turned for a counterattack when the stalker dashed out. But before she pulled the trigger, she had seen the barrage of bullets hitting the door. Now, she turned back, looking for where the shots had come.

"Go on, I'll cover you," Zuri assured.

She had positioned an M4A1 behind one of the willow trees, eyes on the scope.

Azra gave her a moment's gaze. She noticed and yelled:

"GET HIM OUTTA HERE, Azra, I GOT THIS."

Her voice awakened Azra. She continued on her way to the bike. Zuri kept shooting at the door to keep the men inside. However, they had all broken free through the windows on the other side.

Immediately, they spotted Azra leading Dr. Fowler, and a crackle of shots went up in the air. Azra's reflexes immediately went to work, dragging Dr. Fowler along with her. They both landed on the ground just behind the truck. The incoming bullets hit the truck as if dropping a handful of granite on a metal board.

Zuri quickly dismantled the M4A1 and skipped behind the truck.

"GO!" she yelled again.

Azra got on her feet and helped Dr. Fowler up. Zuri had already taken position behind the truck. She opened fire at the men, allowing Azra to put Dr. Fowler on her bike.

Ready to go, she gazed at Zuri, gratitude in her eyes. "Don't get killed."

Zuri gave a sideways smile and set her eyes back at the scope.

Azra revved the bike and then turned to Zuri again. "I'll be waiting at Physician's Redwood."

Zuri glanced at her as she hit the gear and zoomed off.

One of the men stormed out through the entrance and mounted on the bike while the rest engaged Zuri in a war of bullets.

Zuri went to the other side of the truck – a good vantage point. As the man fired up the engine, she shot at him. The bullets clanked against the metal parts of the bike. He dove off, reaching for the door. Zuri had been keeping tabs on Azra to understand that she hardly killed her enemies. She would rather incapacitate them. She herself fought by this code.

A bullet had broken through the bike's fuel tank. As fuel leaked through, Zuri fired one more shot, igniting it. The bike exploded, throwing bits of flame around it and igniting more of the fuel. The men did not stop shooting at the truck.

But at this time, Zuri began to withdraw. The men followed her, shooting sporadically and from both sides. Sparks punctuated the dark, and a ceremony of gunshots broke the air. With bullets flying in every direction, Zuri could have been overwhelmed. But she stood her ground, bearing the same spirit as Azra.

She ran and took cover behind the willow tree. A trail of bullets spattered on the tree just as she leaned against it. Her chest rose and fell heavily as she breathed hard. She took out a magazine from her jacket and loaded her rifle. She cocked it and held it to her chest, taking deep, relaxing breaths.

Immediately, her head poked out of the cover; the men opened fire. She withdrew at once. Her breathing spiked once again. The men had their eyes on the tree – any move she made would have them shooting ceaselessly. She was trapped.

She looked around her. A stick lay next to her feet. She cautiously picked it up and hurled it at the truck. The men opened fire at the truck. She took aim, eyes keen on the target. Focus on the same frequency as the wind. And with a sniper's precision, she shot at one of the men. The bullet whizzed through the air, unwavering, pointing straight at the target. In less than a second, it tore through the man's bicep. He yelled as pangs of pain shredded his nerves.

That moment of distraction afforded Zuri some time to escape. Other gang members continued to shoot at her nonetheless, but she blended well with darkness.

After about a minute, a bike broke off some distance away. The gang went after it, shooting. But their speed was no match for a Suzuki GSX-R1000.

BASE

zra had taken Dr. Fowler home.

"I did this for old time's sake. And no matter what happened between us, I still trust you will not betray me."

She said these words to him upon dropping him off at his house. Dr. Fowler had only stared at her, not sure of what to say.

Now, she waited at the foot of Physician's Redwood, wrapped in the arms of darkness. Her thoughts were with Zuri. She hoped she hadn't been killed or captured. She would have to look for her if she waited 3 more minutes.

But even before the first minute elapsed, a parallel beam pierced the darkness, revealing Azra and the giant redwood behind her. Azra let off a breath of relief.

Zuri turned off the light as she approached the tree. A blend of thoughts clogged her mind. But in all, she hoped she had earned the right to be a part of Azra's crusade.

Zuri disembarked and walked up to Azra.

"I'm sorry for keeping you waiting. I was…"

Azra snapped her explanation with a "thank you."

Zuri swallowed back the rest of the words and nodded lightly.

"Why do you try so hard to be part of this?" Azra questioned.

"I already told you: I just wanna give my life a meaning. I want to be a part of something that helps shape the society we all want."

Azra had heard that before, but she wanted more. "It's a journey of no return. Even if you quit later, it'll still be a part of you. It can influence your mental state negatively. You don't want that for yourself."

"I do. No pain, no gain. In the end, it'll be worth it."

Azra could barely see her eyes in the dark, but the tone of her voice was that of total resolve.

"I'm making plans to set up a base," she revealed. "I just haven't found the right place yet."

"I have a place suitable for operations. You'll like it."

"Where?"

"It's a bunker 2km from Regent Base, just before Lonely Woods."

Azra cocked a brow. "You own it?"

"My grandma used to sell rifles illegally to the black folks decades ago. The bunker was her warehouse. I inherited it."

It made sense to Azra. A base away from home would be rewarding. "Can you take me to it?"

"Of course, anytime!"

She heaved a deep breath as though she had feared Zuri would disagree.

"Here, 12 pm, tomorrow. That okay?"

"Sure!"

Azra stretched forth her hand, and Zuri wasted no time locking in, all the while staring at each other.

She felt Zuri's hand shaking. A smile crinkled the corners of her mouth. That was her squealing with excitement.

* * *

Jasmine had snuck back into her house as usual. She had checked on her kids first before joining Michael in bed. He had appeared to be deeply asleep, but he revealed the contrary at 5 a.m.

"Your inexplicable absences are not good for the children, honey," he reproved.

Jasmine rubbed on her sleepy eyes. Michael had woken her up just when she was about to reach her REM stage.

Her eyes darted at the question. "What are you talking about?"

"You know what I'm talking about. One minute, you're here; the next, you're not. And this happens more often at night. Do you mind telling me what's going on?"

Michael spoke with a blend of anger and concern in his voice.

Jasmine's eyes fluttered. But she feigned ignorance. "I have no idea what you're talking about. I'm always here for my family anytime."

"No, you're not! Melissa wanted you to help her with her math homework. We looked for you everywhere…"

"I only stepped out to see a friend."

"At 11:45 pm? Say something else, please."

"There's nothing going on, honey. I'm fine…"

Michael's jaws tightened. "If nothing's going on like you claim, then why did you sneak back into the room last night?"

"Sneak back? I don't understand."

"I was awake when you came in. I noticed the uncanny movements you made. The other day, I smelt blood in the room. You seem to have been hiding something lately."

Jasmine's chest dropped with a deep breath. She surmised that this moment had the propensity to erupt into a fierce argument. It was best she approached it cautiously.

"Sometimes I just want to step out and get some fresh air like the therapist advised. There's nothing going on, honey. It's the truth. I noticed you were exhausted last night. I didn't want to disturb your sleep. We both agreed to do Melissa's homework this morning. I didn't think she would revisit it last night."

She slid her hand across his shoulder. He didn't seem to buy her explanation - the reason for the frown on his face.

She shook him lightly. "I am fine, honey. Don't get yourself worked up over nothing…"

Azra was born three months ago. Since then, Jasmine has tried not to let her get in the way. Although she seems to be lagging lately, the vision of a better society for her children drives her even deeper.

* * *

Regent Base was an expanse of space. The central part of the base was occupied by a cathedral-sized building. The broken windows, mosses, and creeping plants growing on it told of a decades-old structure.

A windy pathway crossed the space for hundreds of meters. It is bordered by tall fir trees housing flocks of birds. Azra and Zuri walked through this pathway.

They may not be in their nightly costume, but Azra knew their invasion of the warehouse last night might have rattled the wrong people. No one else knew her true identity except Dr. Fowler and Zuri. Even so, she must always watch her back.

"Does anyone live there?" She pointed at the ancient building.

"No," Zuri answered. "I don't know the history of the place, but I know it's been abandoned for decades."

Azra's investigative eyes were everywhere. She wanted to be sure it was safe out here. But with these tents and cabins scattered around the base, she wasn't so sure.

The fir trees on both sides provided shade from the burning heat. Relaxing was the wind as the branches swayed. The birds didn't stop chirping and flapping from one treetop to another. The ground itself was a mess. Azra could see the trees of Lonely Woods about a kilometer away. It told her of how close they were to the bunker.

"Is there another way to the bunker?"

Zuri tucked her hair behind her ear. "Yeah, through Lonely Woods!"

Azra nodded and glanced skyward. It was like a party going on at the treetops. The birds sang and whistled blissfully. Leaves dropped on the ground like crumbs from a king's table. Some of them landed on the ladies' hair. Now, it seemed like some floral decoration.

Azra moved her eyes between a boulder and the cabin next to it. "Uh, where's the bunker?"

"Behind the cabin," Zuri answered assuredly.

Beyond the pathway was the cabin and the boulder next to it. Lonely Woods was only a few meters away. Yet, there was nothing to prove that a bunker was underground. Azra had expected to see a doorway or something. But it was a level ground before the woods.

That, however, made the place even more mysterious and almost impossible to find.

They walked between the mold-grown rock and the cabin. Azra looked through the cabin window. A small, square table broken at the center laid on its side. A rope the size of that used for anchoring in a harbor hung down from the roof. A table and a rope: Azra thought there was a bad combination of murder and suicide. She couldn't help but pinch her nostrils as the smell of decaying wood wafted through them.

A few feet away from the cabin, Zuri stopped. "Here."

Azra looked at the spot she pointed at. Curiosity danced in her eyes.

Zuri bent at her waist and curled her fingers around an invisible handle. She pulled on it, revealing a staircase. A light cloud of dust came through the opening alongside the scrunchy sound of leaves falling off the cover. Azra waved her hand across her nose.

However, she noticed that most of the leaves on the cover did not fall off. That was strange! "Are these leaves sewn onto the cover or something?" she inquired.

"Something like that. They help conceal the cover. Come on…"

Satisfying!

Azra took one step at a time down the staircase. It was dark, and her eyes were wide open to collect as much light as possible. But after Zuri carefully closed back the cover, she went before her and pulled on a lever hung on the wall. The grating sound it made echoed down the bunker.

The lights reveal a barren space.

"Here we are!" Zuri spread her arms while taking note of the look on Azra's face.

It was plain, yet convincing that she liked it. She went closer to the wall. The drawings were familiar - those of guns, skulls and crossbones, bullets, and baseball caps. A couple of writings hung here and there. One of which read:

"The blacks live on!"

Azra sighed. "Looks like your granny was an advocate for the blacks."

"She was. Her husband was a black man."

"Oh…!"

Azra turned to the other side of the bunker. Her eyes fell on a door almost half the size of a regular door.

"Where does that lead to?" she pointed.

"See for yourself…"

Zuri led her to the door. Her skin flushed at the low temperature in the bunker. Her nose flared at the smell of dust like that on the first day of rain.

As Zuri opened the door, the same smell and even a lower temperature hit her senses. Stone walls on both sides bordered the windy pathway that led to another staircase. Beside the staircase was another narrow path leading toward the same opening. Azra thought it was designed for her bike.

"Emergency exit!" Zuri gestured.

Azra cocked a brow as she looked up and back at the staircase.

They both walked out to the central stage. Azra was still taking in the new setting.

"So… what do you think?" Zuri inquired hopefully.

"Not bad. We just need to set it up…"

"Yeah. We can have the controls somewhere there, the central table here, and others…" Zuri spoke enthusiastically, gesturing all the while.

Azra surveyed the whole place once again. "I'll go home and draw out all that we need. You should do the same, too, just so we don't miss anything, and send it to me. I'll place an order for them."

"I bet you wouldn't like a change of costume?"

Azra shrugged. "Maybe something a little more sophisticated."

Zuri nodded.

Azra took out her phone and tapped on it. "My goodness! I should go get my kids from school."

She stormed toward the staircase, slicking strands of her hair down with her hand. Zuri followed her.

The lights soon went out, and the cover thudded shut.

Jasmine hurried through the school gate, panting for breath. She was 30 minutes late and hoped Michael hadn't come to take them. It would be another opportunity to rub how careless she had become on her face.

Swift and relentless, her legs carried her slim frame up the staircase. A few feet away from the door, she spotted Melissa's teacher coming through.

"Hello, Mrs. Jasmine," the teacher greeted first, with a light smile on her face.

"Mrs. Hemingway, I'm so sorry. I should have been here earlier."

"It's okay. We're all guilty of lateness. But you don't have to worry. Someone already took them home."

Jasmine skipped a breath. Eyes wide, she stared at the chubby lady in front of her. "Someone?"

"Yes. Your kids, Melissa and Audrey, waited by the gate after school. After a few minutes, a car drove by, and they both went in. I didn't see the face of the driver, but I think it was your husband."

"Why?"

"The kids went into the car without hesitation. It was obvious they knew and trusted the driver. He didn't have to come out of the car."

Jasmine was quiet, looking past Mrs. Hemingway to the mural of Albert Einstein behind her. Her mind had drifted off. She feared the man in the car might not be Michael…

"Excuse me, Mrs. Jasmine." Mrs. Hemingway continued on her way, breaking the thoughts in her mind.

If not Michael, then who could it be?

There was only one way to find out.

She cascaded down the staircase toward the gate, her hair bouncing all the while.

Her taxi driver was lazy and slow—slower than the earth orbiting the sun. But it was all in her head. The man drove at the normal speed limit. She wished she had been the one driving. She would have covered the 1km distance in less than 2 minutes.

The taxi soon pulled over in front of her bungalow. Having settled the driver, she dashed out of the car. Her anxiety had doubled over time. Illusions like those of a kid who had just completed 3 seasons of a horror movie had clouded her mind.

She flung the door open.

"Mummy!" Audrey skipped from the chair and hugged her.

Melissa had just come through the kitchen door, carrying a cup of milk. "Mummy!"

Jasmine hugged her too and rubbed on their hair affectionately. A deep breath had escaped her upon seeing them.

"Are you okay, honey?" she inquired, bringing her height to theirs.

"Yes, mummy. Daddy sent a driver to come pick us up from school."

Jasmine's eyes darted. "A driver?"

"Yes, mummy."

"Did he tell you what his name is?"

"No. He said he was friends with you and Daddy."

Jasmine was drifting away again, but she quickly recognized it. A smile stretched the corners of her mouth.

"All right, guys. You go to your room now, okay? Mummy wants to take care of something. I'll be with you shortly."

"Okay, mummy."

Melissa led Audrey up the stairs, sipping on her milk.

Jasmine watched them for a while before padding to the chair. It groaned under her weight.

Michael didn't have a driver. Even if he did, he would have called her to be sure she hadn't taken the kids home. Even more suspicious was the so-called driver claiming to be friends with her and her husband, yet not telling the kids his name. Asking Michael about him would arouse suspicions. She would have to warn her kids against such unverified friends or drivers.

* * *

In the depths of night, a sense of foreboding hung in the still air. As crickets buzzed, the threat resounded even louder. Somehow, Jasmine could feel it; she could hear it, but she paid no attention to it.

Sitting at the table in her room, she made a list of all that was needed in her new base. Zuri had sent hers, too, most of which were items for tech-savvy experts. The list gathered around a hundred thousand dollars or more. For a digital marketer, it was almost impossible to come up with such an amount of money in a short time. But covered by Dr. Fowler's insurance, it was a fair trade.

Michael cuddled his pillow hard as he slept. Jasmine did not tell him about the man who brought the kids back from school. She hoped they didn't either.

She went through the list one more time and folded the paper into a cylindrical shape. Then, she crouched and took out a piece of the floorboard. Michael probably didn't know about this lost piece.

Inside the hole was what looked like a jewelry box. She slid the paper through a pocket in the box and closed it.

Having covered the hole, she got on her feet and stretched like a hard rubber. Halfway through a yawn, she noticed a shadow flit past her window.

Her mouth snapped shut along with the space between her brows. She strode to the window and looked through.

She saw a figure cross the edge of the building to the front. Their movements were fluid and decisive. Whoever it was certainly knew what they had come to do.

Jasmine dashed out of the room. In a moment, she was making her way down the stairs. She padded stealthily, but the sound of her flip flop and the creaks of floorboards underfoot announced her coming to a careful listener. Her eyes shifted from one window to another. It seemed she had lost the figure.

Her cautious steps brought her to the door. She leaned her ear on it. Only the buzzing of crickets filtered through. The silence of the night lingered in the background.

Her fingers wrapped around the handle. The hinges grated as she turned it and opened the door. Her head came first. Her eyes scanned the surroundings. There was no sign of the figure anywhere. However, they fell on a piece of paper tucked down the flower pot by the door.

She sized up the area one more time and then went for the paper.

She picked it up cautiously and unfolded it.

"You dare interfere in my business! I'll make you pay!"

Jasmine read the words again and again. She looked around, and the question came back: "Who could this be?"

She could tell the interference, whoever it was, meant she was rescuing Dr. Fowler. Could it be the driver the kids were talking about? Her face darkened even more. And how did they know it was her? How did they know where she lived? Only Dr. Fowler and now Zuri knew her true identity. Could either of them have betrayed her?

She winced and placed her hand on her forehead. It had become foggy, causing her a headache. She tucked the paper down her pajamas and went back inside. All she needed was Pantorex, the drug prescribed by her therapist, Dr. Krishna. It was meant to calm her anxiety and help her sleep better. But perhaps she needed to do a little more digging on the drug.

AQUA

The orders had arrived. A new base had been set up. Zuri saw to it. Supercomputers, tracking devices, technical consoles, display and analytical screens, security systems, different types of firearms, bullets, explosives, and a lot more. The once-empty bunker was now a top sophisticated base. Zuri tagged it, 'The BC base.' 'B' for Azra, 'C' for Crusade.

She had just given Azra a rundown of every part of the base - from the controls to the glass wardrobe that housed her costume.

Azra had brought her bike and every other item in the basement to her house. They had a new home now. Zuri had set them up, too.

"It's amazing," she had commented while checking out the section for the rifles.

Now, Zuri sat at the control desk, hacking into the security cameras of the city's most popular spots. Azra was still exploring the base.

"Uh… Azra, there's something I'd like you to see…"

Azra moved over to the control desk at once. "What is it?"

"I think there's a robbery going on at Wonder City Bank. Look," she pointed at the location pin, "the heat wave spreading out indicates there are gunshots in the area…"

"Were you able to infiltrate the security cameras?"

"Yeah…" She turned the swivel chair and took hold of the mouse. She clicked on it, and different bank sections were displayed in a tile format. "Here…"

The first tile showed the bank's hallway. The second showed the banking hall. The bankers and customers lay on the floor. Two men held a gun over them.

Azra dashed off to the wardrobe. "I have to get there as quickly as possible."

"You got your Kawasaki Ninja. And by the way," she swiveled around in the chair to face Azra. I ramped up the calibrations, hoping you could handle the speed.

"Very thoughtful!"

In two minutes, Azra had suited up. She had the intercom plugged to her ear. She didn't need a rifle - just one or two pistols and knives tucked down her pants.

She went for the bike. It felt somewhat lighter as she revved it. The growls echoed throughout the bunker. It would be one disadvantage they would have to endure until Zuri found a better place for the bike.

"I like this," Azra commented, a smile hovering on her lips.

"I knew you would."

Azra fired it one more time and then rode off toward the exit.

At ground level, the darkness of night permeated the space. The silence was broken by bats screeching and hawks cawing. The cries of monkeys could also be heard from Lonely Woods. Azra took the path through Regent Base. The only source of light was the bike's headlamps piercing the darkness over a hundred meters or more.

Azra traced her way out of Regent Base to the road. Wonder City Bank it was!

At 1 am, she had the road to herself. She swayed past some cars and other bikes, nonetheless. She had loosened her hair. A new look for the baddie. And now it flew and ruffled in the wind like a model with a photo shoot.

She could hear the police siren in the distance. If they could handle the problem, it would be unnecessary interference.

"Juli, what's going on at the bank?" she inquired via the intercom.

"Robbers gathering as much money as they could." She chuckled.

"Casualties?"

"None yet."

"How about the police?"

"At the scene, still looking for a way in. I think the robbers are keeping the people inside as hostages…"

"What?!"

"Yeah. The police are probably trying to negotiate."

Azra swung past an SUV and dashed through an alleyway.

"What about the robbers? Do you have any idea how many they are?"

Zuri did not answer immediately. Azra thought she was probably counting. She stumbled out of the alleyway, drove down a street, and rounded a rotary. This side of the road led straight to WCB.

"5 of them," Zuri answered. "3 are with the hostages, and the other 2 are in the vault with the manager."

"What is the best way through the banking hall?"

"The main entrance, for the sake of the hostages."

"All right…"

Azra fired on.

From a distance, she saw police officers gathered at the premises. Siren lights flashed across the dark sky. The shootout Zuri was talking about obviously lasted for a short time.

She parked behind a corner shop several meters away.

"At the scene now," she reported as she made her way toward the bank.

"I know," Zuri replied. "I had a tracker installed in the bike."

Azra rolled her eyes. "Isn't that a little invasive?"

"I'm sorry if it is. But I thought It'd help me keep track of your location in case anything goes wrong…"

She set the bike on lockdown. It beeped and flashed red lights.

Azra did not argue her reason. It was legit.

She walked down the road, meandering through dark corners. Looking at the bank, it didn't seem like any progress had been made toward catching the robbers. She herself would have to be cautious to avoid any casualties.

Having gotten close enough, she stopped, hidden in a dark shade. She inhaled deeply and closed her eyes. A gust of wind blew against her hair, releasing the energy around her. Her mind became one with nature, and her senses aligned with the elements.

After a moment, the glob of water on the ground shook as though it was boiling. That gurgling sound could be heard within the area and beyond.

It lasted for a few seconds. The glob of water settled again. Azra opened her eyes.

At once, she levitated off the ground and launched herself over the premises like a missile. Without a cape on, she looked more like a javelin. Her slim frame looked like it was naturally streamlined for this purpose. She cut through the air the same way a missile would. Only a few eyes saw her jetting across.

In mid-air, she raised her hands. Every drop of water in the area, as far as 100 meters wide, coalesced into a giant ball that was twice as large as a boulder. It was like a naked fish tank. The water swirled at nearly a hundred revolutions per minute. Those who saw it left their mouths open in astonishment.

At a speed of 40mph, it flew across the sky and crashed against the door. The glass blasted into smithereens like it was struck with a sledgehammer. The shattering sound was like that of two trucks colliding at top speed. The shards clinked rhythmically as they dropped on the floor - some of them sliced through hostages sitting on the floor of the banking hall.

The robbers had fallen back at the force of the explosion, unable to keep their feet on the ground. The other two, with the manager, had just arrived at the central hall when the crash occurred. The vibrations had shaken the bags and guns off their hands.

Almost everyone was drenched, including the robbers, who were now trying to get back on their feet and regain control of the situation.

Azra landed in the banking hall. Before the robbers achieved a firm grip on their guns, she zipped past the hostages in a flash and disarmed them. It happened so fast that they had no idea they had lost their guns until she returned to her initial position.

"Get on your knees now!" She leveled a gun at them. They were reluctant at first, but she barked, "NOW!"

They all fell on their knees at once, dripping with water.

She glanced at the hostages. "Get outta here, all of you. GO!"

Everyone scrambled to their feet, dripping with water. Quickly, they shuffled out of the bank. Azra had her eyes on the robbers all the while.

Immediately, the police saw them coming out; some of them guided their way, and the rest stormed into the bank and apprehended the robbers. The guns were on the floor when Azra left the bank.

"Hey!" an officer called.

But she was already in the air and off to where she parked her bike.

"That was easy!" Zuri commented.

"Not as you think." Azra mounted her bike. "Words on the street?"

"No. All clear!"

"Good. Back to base!"

While Azra was on her way, Zuri scanned through the city maps and the security cameras. The cameras at the Global Research Facility showed police vehicles driving in. Scientists at the facility were standing at the main entrance. It appeared something had happened.

Azra soon arrived at the base. "I need to get back home." She moved over to the wardrobe.

"I think you should see this first," Zuri called.

"What is it?" She walked to the control desk.

"I think something happened at Global Research. The police just arrived."

Azra gazed at the screen, the lights reflecting on her face. "Maybe they lost someone that was meant to be used for a scientific test. It's no big deal..."

"I think it's more than that. These scientists wouldn't be standing at the entrance if that were the case."

Despite Zuri's words, Azra found nothing worth her attention on the screen. To her, it was probably a bad day at the Global Research Facility.

"I should get going."

But as she turned, her eyes fell on the TV hung on the wall. A report was going on, and footage similar to that on Zuri's screen was playing in the background.

"Turn up the volume."

Zuri swiveled around. She picked up the remote quickly upon seeing the report.

"...the abduction took place between 1:27 am and 1:54 am. Drs. Mathew and Alfred are two of the top scientists in the state. It leaves everyone wondering who could be responsible for their abduction. However, the rumor going around suggests that Azra might be involved in their abduction. This is because a mask similar to hers was found at the scene. The police have commenced investigations. It is hoped that sooner rather than later, they will come up with information regarding the whereabouts of the scientists..."

"What?" Azra's face scrunched up. "Is someone trying to set me up or something?"

"I think the robbery at Wonder City Bank was part of it," Zuri suggested.

"How?"

"It was merely a distraction from the main event."

Azra processed this information. It made some sense. Whoever set it up knew she would be busy trying to save the day at the bank while they carried out the abduction.

"I need to find this person before they destroy the good image I've managed to build in a few months."

Zuri glanced at the TV again. The report was still going on - an officer was being interviewed by the press at this time. But she had turned down the volume.

"But why are they going after top scientists? First, it was Dr. Fowler, and now these two. What exactly do they want?"

"Powers, I guess."

"What kind of powers?" Zuri grimaced.

"They think the scientists can help them acquire some superpowers. I must warn my husband at once. He's a top scientist, too."

She returned to the wardrobe to change back to her pajamas. Zuri got back to the systems.

THERAPIST

Jasmine sat by the table, her left arm resting on it. She crossed her right leg over the left, looking around the office as though it was her first time here. The table and shelf were of thick mahogany with a sleek red-brown finish. She was certain her data was one of those in the computer on the table. And she was here to give some more.

The door snapped and creaked open. Considering how noisy it was, a thief would find such a door annoying. Dr. Krishna came through, carrying a file in her hand.

"My apologies, Mrs. Jasmine. I had an urgent matter to attend to." She dropped the file on the table and tapped on a few keys on her computer. She came and sat on the chair opposite Jasmine, who had yet to utter a word. "You don't look happy. What's wrong?" she asked.

Jasmine gazed at her as if to be sure she was talking to the right person. "Have you ever felt like your work is getting in the way of your relationship?"

Dr. Krishna scratched the back of her ear and cleared her throat. "I am not in a relationship. Actually, my last relationship ended because I let my work get in the way."

"What do you mean?"

"As a psychologist and a perfectionist, I wanted a perfect relationship. He did his best because he loved me deeply. But he got sick of my choking demands and jilted. Then I realized there could never be anything like a perfect relationship."

"It means that even in marriage, it can never be perfect. Mistakes are normal, right?”

“Depends on the kind of mistakes you’re talking about and how many times one repeats the same mistakes.”

Jasmine recoiled and looked away, processing what Dr. Krishna had just said.

“You mind telling me what’s going on?” asked Dr. Krishna.

Jasmine’s feeble gaze fell back on her therapist. “A part of me tends to come between my family and me.”

“Is this part of you an ailment, a habit, or someone?”

“Call it a habit.”

“Hmm… does this habit influence the way you communicate with your family?”

“No.”

“And did you talk to your husband about it?”

“No.”

“Why?”

“It’s personal.”

“Okay.” Dr. Krishna exhaled deeply, picking up a more cheerful expression. “You should understand that you’re not alone in this. Sometimes, we become so attached to something that it steals us from our loved ones. If they love us, they will complain, hoping we’ll adjust. If we value their presence in our lives, we’ll find a way to solve the problem.”

Jasmine sighed. Her brain worked the math.

“You know what that part of you is. Look out for where the problem lies and a possible solution. If whatever it is demands as much time as your family, look for a way to balance it.”

Jasmine gazed at the flower vase behind her, but her mind was processing her advice. It seemed like the right thing to do. Telling her husband about it was never an option. So, best it would be if she could find a balance for both parts of her life.

After her time with her therapist, Jasmine came out of the office building. It was 11 a.m., yet the sun burned like it was 2 p.m. Heat waves could be seen just above glasses and aluminum objects. She took out a pair of sunshades and put them on. Now, she walked toward her car parked in the space.

Those who had encountered her as Azra might be able to recognize her. She had the same bad-girl charisma and aura. Her gait and waist swung with a rhythm. With hair as black as tar and flailing in the wind, it was hard to believe she was a mother of two.

A few steps away from her car, she heard her name:

"Hey, Jasmine."

She turned sharply. Her friend Susan was walking toward her in a formal red dress. It appeared she had come for a business meeting.

They had been close friends since high school and had managed to remain so through the years. However, it appeared that the friendship had hit rock bottom. Jasmine thought it was probably what she wanted to talk about.

"Hi Su, been a while," Jasmine responded, resting her hand on the roof of her BMW.

"Indeed! You don't call and hardly answer mine. You don't reply to my messages either. And when I visit, you're hardly ever around. Do you mind telling me what's going on?"

Jasmine scratched her hair with her key. She had already lost interest in the conversation before it even began.

"I'm trying to take care of a problem, Su. Shit's eating into my time. Forgive me."

"And when did you start calling only when you're free? How personal is the problem that you cannot share it with your closest friend?"

"Pretty personal!"

"Yeah, 'cause it's written all over you."

"Is it?"

"Of course, it is. You look like you haven't had a good sleep in months."

Jasmine dabbed her cheeks rather remorsefully. Susan simply gazed at her, but it was for a moment.

"I have to go now. Someone's waiting for me."

"Me too. I need to go get my kids from school."

"You take care of whatever the problem is and call me. And in case you need someone to talk to, you know you always got my ears."

Jasmine smiled genially. "I know. Thank you."

Susan walked past her, patting her shoulder. Jasmine took a deep breath, pouting her lips, and got into her car.

As she put on her seatbelt, she looked at her watch. It was already 10 minutes before 2 pm. It should take 7 minutes max to get to Kingsbury High School. She would wait willingly if she got there earlier, giving the so-called driver no chance.

She pulled on the gear lever and reversed the car.

The road to the school was usually free from heavy traffic—it was a ring road, after all. Jasmine drove slightly above the normal speed limit. She overtook a few cars on her way, hoping it would continue that way until she got to the school.

But the BMW began to decelerate. There was traffic on the ring road, and cars lined up like a cortege. Jasmine got to the point and stopped.

"Shit!" She slammed her hand on the steering wheel with clenched teeth.

She looked at her watch again. Three minutes had gone by already. Her breathing was getting elevated, as defined by her chest inflating and deflating in short, steady seconds. She had no idea what had caused the traffic but hoped it relieved itself soon.

While she waited, her mind drifted off to the letter she had received last night. Could it be the same person trying to destroy her reputation? Could it be the driver? She looked down at the gear case and took her phone.

She wanted to call Dr. Fowler. But halfway through it, she developed a cold feeling. Nevertheless, she had dialed the number already. She prayed it didn't ring. And no, it didn't, and she didn't bother to drop a voicemail.

Just as she dropped the phone, cars began to move. Six minutes had passed. Jasmine revved the engine lightly and followed up. The road soon freed up, and the BMW was up and running again.

However, by the time Jasmine arrived at the school, her kids had already been picked up.

"I saw a man lead them into the car," Audrey's teacher reported.

Jasmine would have to talk to the principal and the teachers involved. Only the kids' parents should be allowed to take them – no one else. This time, she decided to talk to her husband about it.

THE CLINIC

Melissa and Audrey were safe at home. When Jasmine arrived, they were playing video games. She had asked them about the man who had brought them home.

"He said he was your brother, our uncle," Melissa had answered.

Jasmine had had enough of the lies. With her hands on their shoulders, he had warned them:

"Henceforth, only your dad and I are allowed to pick you up from school – no one else, no matter who they claim they are. If you don't see your dad or myself, do not get into the car, you understand?"

"But why, mummy? Our uncle was nice to us," Audrey had protested.

"He's dangerous, honey. He's only being nice so he can lure you out and hurt you. You don't want to be hurt, do you?"

The little boy had nodded.

"Good!"

Melissa seemed to have understood the message quite clearly.

"Remember, only your father and I, no one else."

Jasmine had made sure to remind them of the warning. She would discuss it with their father, who would, in turn, talk to the principal or teachers about it, or she would do it herself.

Michael got back from work at 12 am. The kids had gone to bed at this time. Jasmine waited for him to get a shower so they could talk. However, she stepped out of the house to get some fresh air and survey the premises for possible invasion like she usually did.

Stars studded the sky like white dots on a black background, glinting in brilliant iridescence. Jasmine kept glancing skyward as she investigated the area. The serene atmosphere appeared to have drifted from the seaside. A neighbor's dog barking in the distance broke the silence of the night, but that didn't make it less beautiful.

She went to the left side of the building, through the back to the right, and back to the front – her investigative eyes reaching every corner. All clear! A peaceful night to set things right, she thought.

Jasmine wanted to be out here for as long as possible. She wanted just to stand around and let the fresh air rejuvenate her senses. After all, there was nothing to do at the base tonight. But sleep was starting to creep in, and she needed to talk with her husband about the kids.

She took a shot of the sky again and went back inside. The locks snapped shut. She switched off the lights and plodded up the staircase.

As she opened the door to her room, she saw Michael quickly shove a piece of paper into his pocket. He had done it so frantically that a part of the paper stuck out. He noticed it and pushed it in, looking rather awkward.

"What are you hiding?" Jasmine inquired, coming closer.

"Nothing." Michael's voice quivered.

"You know that's not true, honey."

"I'm not hiding anything." He closed the briefcase on the bed and took it to the wardrobe.

Jasmine's eyes followed his movements. She could already tell he was not ready to divulge what it was to her. She was not going to ask him again, anyway. She flicked it off as if nothing happened and got on the bed.

"There's something I want us to talk about, darling."

"What is it about?"

She saw him take out the paper, throw it into his briefcase, and then lock it, but she kept her pretense.

"It's about the kids…"

* * *

The day started normally. Michael agreed to speak with the principal of Kingsbury and the teachers involved with his children. As per the regular routine, he took them to school.

Jasmine didn't get the opportunity to see what was written on the paper he was hiding. It couldn't have been a scientific formula. Or was it a divorce paper? Michael would definitely have talked to her about it. What, then, was it?

As more thoughts came into her head, curiosity heightened. But the paper had been in his briefcase all through the night. For now, there was nothing she could do about it.

She got a job this morning. Without delay, she was already on it, hoping to complete it before dusk. While on it, she spared some time to check out the papers. According to them, the rumor of her being responsible for the abduction still lingered. And the police were looking forward to uncovering Azra's identity.

She wouldn't deny she felt a hint of anxiety inside of her. It would all come to nothing if she was discovered. Dr. Fowler wouldn't betray her. She didn't think Zuri would either. What about the man that brought her the letter?"

It soon became a battle between anxiety and focus. Finding this ghost would be the best thing to ever happen to her in a long time.

At around 5 p.m., she was still working on the client's project. She had managed to regain concentration, and bringing her children back herself contributed to her peace of mind.

While she prepared slides, her phone beeped. She glanced at it and then set her eyes back on the computer screen. But then, something already caught her attention. It was a text message from Dr. Fowler.

Jasmine took the phone and opened the message:

"Some criminals are planning to attack New Haven Clinic tonight. I believe they want to steal a newborn from the clinic. We may not be friends anymore, but I trust you can do something. Time is 11 pm."

Jasmine stared at the message but did not read any part of it. Questions sprouted like seeds in her head—questions she had yet to get answers to if she ever would. She would definitely be at the clinic before 11 p.m.

She returned to the project she was working on. But her mind kept shifting back and forth. The words continued to resound in her head. Why would anyone want to abduct a baby? If only she could mount 24-hour surveillance on the clinic.

She picked up her phone and texted Zuri:

"I need you to hack into New Haven Clinic's security system. Keep a close eye on it until I report to base."

She dropped the phone and interlocked her fingers beneath her jaw. Things were fast spiraling out of control in a city she swore to protect. She had a goal: finding whoever it was behind the plans.

* * *

"Why did you ask me to keep an eye on the clinic?" Zuri inquired, propping herself up on her elbow.

Azra had put her kids to bed before arriving at the base at 9 pm. Michael had called to inform her that he would not return home tonight. She did not read any meaning to it. But somewhere in her mind, a weird thought was cultivated.

"Got a message from Dr. Fowler," Azra answered.

"Dr. Fowler?" Zuri glanced up at her, confused.

"Yes. It was about an attack. He believes some criminals want to steal a newborn."

"Oh my god! A baby? For what?"

"I don't know."

Zuri glanced at the four parts of the screen. One part showed the nurses at the lounge, the other part showed the doctor on a ward round, and the last two tiles showed the entrance to the clinic and the security checkpoint.

"You knew Dr. Fowler before now?" Zuri questioned.

It was as though the question flitted past Azra. A long silence simmered. It was a bit of a hard decision to let Zuri into her past. Or maybe she could simply answer a 'yes.' But although it looked like a 'yes-or-no' question, it wasn't actually one.

"He took care of me when I first learned about my powers. He made me realize they could be used for the greater good."

Zuri nodded. "I see. Then it's probably the reason he was abducted."

"Yes. They wanted to extract information about me from him."

Zuri was quiet, but it was for a moment. "It means your alter ego knows about your relationship with him. Do you have any idea who it could be?"

"No. We did everything possible to keep it a secret. Not even my younger brother, Clark, knows about us."

"Who could this imposter be then?"

That was a question Azra had no answer to for now. She padded to the wardrobe for a change. Zuri brought her attention back to the screen.

In a few minutes, Azra emerged in her usual brown leather pants and jacket – half her face hidden in a brown mask.

"I'm still working on a new suit. Trust me, you're gonna love it," intoned Zuri as she swiveled about, with an enthusiastic smile crinkling her face.

"I'm looking forward to it." Azra put the finishing touches on it and then took the bike key from the analytical table.

"Be careful!" Zuri warned and turned back to the screen.

"I will. Don't take your eyes off the screen."

Once again, the Kawasaki growled, threatening the foundations of the bunker. It climbed the slope and out of the base.

Azra had left an hour earlier. That was because she did not want to rely on the security cameras. The thought of a newborn about to be abducted made her sick. The same person abducted Dr. Fowler and the other two scientists. The same person sent her the letter. The same person was about to abduct a newborn. Her head was foggy as to what they wanted to do with the baby. But Dr. Fowler might have an idea.

She fired on, cutting past cars and other bikes. The wind caused a backward drag on her hair. But the force was too insignificant for that propelling the bike.

In a few minutes, she was standing next to her bike at the foot of a sycamore tree. The tree was about 40m away from the clinic. 20m around the clinic shone nearly as bright as a football stadium. She had to be cautious to cross this area, or she would land herself into more trouble.

"Juli, what's the situation in there?" she asked.

"All clear."

"I'll get closer and see things for myself."

"All right."

Azra knew there were some areas not covered by CCTV, which were the most vulnerable areas. But getting past the security would be a challenge. Three of them were standing at the entrance to the clinic, bordered by a fence of flowers. They turned in every direction.

"Julie, is there a way through?"

"Hold on!"

Azra went closer to cover the distance before the light.

"There's a narrow gap between a trail of flowers on your left."

"Where…?" Azra looked around.

"On your left - far left."

"It's dark here, I can't see anything."

"Look closely, that's the only means."

Azra focused her gaze on the left side, trying not to get distracted by his own thoughts.

"Yeah, I found it."

"Good. Take the road. It'll lead you to the backyard. A good way to bypass the security."

Azra crept toward the flowers. It was to her benefit that this area was poorly illuminated.

As careful as she could, she filtered through the gap, making sure not to ruffle the flowers much. Just like Julie said, it led her to the backyard. There were other buildings here - all of which Azra had no idea what they were for.

Another trail of chrysanthemums traveled from the main and then branched out to the smaller buildings like a tree. Azra had to stay low as there was a window just above her head.

But over a wall of flowers, she saw a head next to a window. She could tell it was that of a man. At first, she thought it was a security guard, but her instincts told her it could be someone else. She leaned against the wall and watched.

After a moment, another man jumped out from the same window. That was definitely not the security, Azra surmised. She could have given them a hot chase, but she didn't want to disturb the peace in the clinic.

She turned back through the gap she had come. From here, she made her way back to her bike. She scanned the surroundings, but there was no sign of the men anywhere.

And just as she mounted her bike, Zuri spoke in the background:

"You got a message from Dr. Fowler."

"Read it."

"I'm sorry, Jasmine. My informant was wrong. Not long ago, the clinic reported the case of a missing baby in its wards. Turns out the theft occurred at around 8 pm."

"What? So, who are these men I just saw leaving the clinic suspiciously?"

"You should go after them. They might have the information we need."

Azra thought they must have gone far. But she decided to look for them, nonetheless.

She turned on the engine and made a U-turn. But by the time she arrived at the other side of the clinic, the men were gone.

"Shit!" she spat and swallowed hard. "They're gone."

Zuri exhaled deeply and then asked: "Now what?"

"Words on the street?"

"All clear!"

"Right! Returning to base."

Azra continued on the same route, hoping she would find the men. Now, that feeling of blame began to creep up her gut. She should have gone after the men. What if they had stolen another baby? She would have caught one of them and extracted information from him. How could she be so foolish?

She drew hard on the accelerator, reaching top speed. Blame and guilt tugged at her heart. She could have done better. The bike had hit its maximum speed limit, whizzing past everything on both sides of the road like it was on its way to the future. Zuri had recorded maximum speed in her systems and had been calling on Azra to slow down. But her guilt blocked off her senses of hearing.

Getting closer to a sharp bend, she slowed down. But she had applied the brakes too late. A pregnant lady was standing on the walkway somewhere ahead. The guilt and blame disappeared instantly at the sight of her. Azra thought she had finally gotten herself into trouble.

However, she pushed hard on the brakes. The lady was buying something from a corner shop, completely oblivious to the danger whizzing closer from behind.

Azra found the horn and tooted it, still pushing down on the brakes. But the lady was slow to react. She only turned and then screamed. At the same time, Azra managed to turn the bike away from her and then zipped off down the road. She kept looking back. Luckily, the lady was still on her feet when she rode out of sight.

The police siren blared in the distance. They were obviously after this psycho on the road.

Azra managed to get to the base without killing anyone.

REUNION

The events of last night brought Jasmine to the dark depths of depression. Zuri emptied her basket of words, trying to make her understand that it wasn't her fault that the men escaped. But all that fell on dry ground.

She had scheduled an appointment with her therapist, and she was in her office as early as 10 a.m.

"You look like you have the weight of the world on your shoulders, Mrs. Jasmine," Dr. Krishna observed, adjusting her bottom on the chair. "You mind telling me what the problem is?"

"I nearly killed an innocent lady last night."

Jasmine may not have committed the crime, but the tone of her voice sounded like she did and was overridden with remorse—not just her voice but the look in her eyes. Dr. Krishna could see the demons in them—Jasmine herself was barely in there.

"Okay. But you didn't, right?" she asked her.

"No. But I saw the fear in her eyes when I almost ran over her. And I let some bad guys get away last night."

Dr. Krishna did not say a word. She just stared at Jasmine. It was a way to let her guilt subside a bit. Jasmine sat with a cold stare in her eyes.

"You said you almost ran over the woman. That means you were overspeeding?"

"Yes. I was angry that I let the bad guys escape."

"Okay. Do you think there could have been a reason why you let the bad guys escape?"

Jasmine's eyes fluttered. And for the first time, she looked away from Dr. Krishna.

"Your silence means there was indeed a reason. So I want to know: do you think this reason was worth it?"

Again, Jasmine did not answer. Her mind had wandered off to the moment that led to everything. Had she gone after those guys, a lot of things could have gone wrong. The staff at the clinic might even think she was responsible for the abduction. Her presence at another crime scene could have given a wrong impression.

"I am no police officer, but I know that sometimes, you have to let the bad guys think they have escaped just to go back and draw out a more effective plan. First, you had a reason for letting them go. And you are convinced that that reason was worth it. Tell me, do you still think it's right to starve yourself of happiness?"

The stiffness on Jasmine's face had relaxed. She had assumed a calm disposition.

"You did not run over the woman. It was only natural that she got scared when she saw you speeding closer. Everyone else would do the same. So look beyond your guilt and realize you have more to be grateful for than be angry at. For the bad guys, there will always be a next time. Forgive yourself..."

Jasmine was grateful for the session. The burden had been lifted—perhaps not completely—but right now, she was in charge of her emotions, in control of her own mind. She took deep breaths throughout the final minutes of the session.

"I should go now," she told Dr. Krishna.

"All right. Have a nice day."

"You too. See you some other time..."

She walked out the door.

Dr. Krishna had a smile on her face all the while. But as the door slammed shut, it faded off like a gust of wind blowing off a lonely wisp of smoke. She assumed a rigid countenance at once.

She stretched forward and took her phone from the table. She tapped frantically on the screen, glancing at the door at short intervals.

Jasmine made her way to her car. Her limbs flailed lighter than before. The city appeared more beautiful, no longer viewed with so much bitterness in her heart.

"Jasmine?" a voice called from behind.

She turned. It was her brother, Clark. He was black and brawny. There was no resemblance between them, or maybe there was: he had that intimidating charisma around his shoulders, just like Jasmine. Only a few had she told that he was her half-brother.

"Clark…!"

They hugged each other.

"Nice to see you again, sis."

"Nice to see you too. What are you doing here?"

"Came to see a friend…"

They exchanged pleasantries outside. But for a proper conversation, Jasmine asked that they talk in the car.

"You know it's been 10 years since I saw you," Jasmine said. Where have you been?"

"Been here and there, tryna survive."

"I couldn't reach you on the phone. Left loads of voicemails that are still unanswered."

Clark nodded. His bulbous nose seemed like it was about to come off. "You know, after the misunderstanding we had over the death of our parents, I wanted to get as far away from you as possible. So I moved to New York. Made a couple of friends who helped me stay on my feet."

"So you were just gonna abandon the only family you have?"

"Honestly, yeah… but I thought about it and realized I was a fool. And for that, I want to apologize for everything I did to you at the death of our parents. I was naive. I was foolish. I realized later on that you couldn't have caused the spark intentionally. I'm sorry."

Jasmine was no longer looking at him but through the windshield. She had been tapping rhythmically on the steering wheel all the while he talked.

But now she faced him: "You were hurting, Clark. I understand your frustration. And maybe I would have done the same, too. We both loved our parents. But all that is in the past now. We have to move on. And I'm glad you have."

"Yeah, I have…" His chest rose and fell with a deep breath. "So… tell me, what have you been up to?"

"Nothing much, just taking care of my kids and saving the world." Jasmine giggled.

"Saving the world? You got some superpowers or something?"

"Yeah."

"Whoa, wait! Are you for real? You got some superpowers?"

"Yes." Jasmine shrugged and giggled excitedly.

"How? You weren't born like that." Clark's face twisted with shock and disbelief. His curious eyes bulged as he gazed down at Jasmine.

"When the sparks occurred, and the whole house went haywire, I was struck too. It wasn't just our parents. I went into a coma for days. I guess my body was going through some modifications during this time. Months later, after extensive tests and evaluations, I realized I had become faster, stronger, and could levitate."

"What? You can levitate?" Clark's brows furrowed.

"Yeah. And I can control water, too."

"Wow! Awesome! You know we can do a lot of things with your powers, right?"

Jasmine laughed softly. "I'm using it for the good of the city. Catching the bad guys and rescuing those held captive, you know, stuff like that."

"Wonderful! I'm proud of you, sis. Pretty sure our parents will be proud of you too."

Jasmine was all smiles and nodding. "Enough of me. Tell me, what about you?"

"Just being me, working at Greenwich Autos."

"For real?"

"Yeah. We're looking to set up a branch here in Wonder City. That's pretty much why I am here. Glad I bumped into you first."

"I'm glad you're doing well for yourself…" She was going for the glove compartment but changed her mind halfway. "Why don't I have your number so I can text you my address?"

"Yeah, sure. I'd like to come to see my niece and nephew someday…"

How much better could the day get for Jasmine? All that guilt she bottled inside of her throughout the night finally got lifted this morning. And like a crown on a jewel, she reunited with her brother. Someone she hadn't seen for 2 years.

Perhaps the events of yesterday happened for a reason, she thought. So she could book an appointment with her therapist and, in the long run, bump into her brother, Clark. It was a marvelous affair.

Now, she drove home, excited. She had no regrets telling him about her powers. She trusted him as much as she did herself. He was her brother, after all. He might be a bit temperamental, but she was certain he could never betray her. And perhaps someday, they might actually work together to save the world.

It all seemed aligned like the stars in winter solstice. Hopefully, it stayed that way.

The day fell short, not giving Jasmine enough time to revel in its bliss. But for the first time in a long while, she felt burden-free. And for that, she was grateful.

Michael had returned from the lab just when the day had turned gray. That was unusual! Melissa and Audrey hung around him playfully. The communication between him and his wife since the night she saw him scruffing a piece of paper behind him had become awkward. Few spoken words. Minimal eye contact. They kept grudges, even though neither admitted it.

But not long after Michael came back, he went out again. And while the kids played video games in their room, Jasmine decided to do something: search for that piece of paper Michael was hiding.

She padded straight to the closet and took out his briefcase. He hadn't changed the pass yet, but it was too easy to unlock.

Inside were papers containing scientific methods and formulas, a pen, and a textbook the size of a pocket dictionary. Jasmine searched every opening in the case but did not find the paper.

She checked every other part of the closet. Nothing! The chest of drawers by the bed. Yes, there! With adrenaline filling up her muscles, she became a little frantic with the search. Her heart pumped almost quicker than her lungs could carry.

She pulled open the drawers and delved in, but she only found clips, staplers, papers, and other items that didn't match what she was looking for.

Giving up was not part of the plan until she thoroughly searched every part of the room. The bed, the pillows, the floorboards, the dressing table, under the shag rug: but she did not find the paper.

Now, she stood at the center of the room with her hands on her waist. She had covered everywhere. If only it were possible to turn the room upside down literally. Somewhere in her mind, a voice hinted that the paper might not be in the room - maybe in the lab. But Jasmine did not want to admit it. And then another voice gave her a clue about the only place she had yet to look.

She tapped her head and stormed back to the wardrobe. The first piece of clothing her hand touched was his trousers. She took it out and shoved her hand down its back pocket. There it was! Crumpled but not torn.

Jasmine spread it out. Only a sentence was written on it:

"Keep the stem cells alive."

Stem cells? Jasmine gazed at the words. What experiment was Michael working on that required stem cells? He was a medical scientist, but this was a bit suspicious to Jasmine. And why was he hiding the paper since it was just a sentence? A myriad of possible reasons clustered in her head.

She put the paper back in her pocket and then reached for her laptop. She dropped her weight on the chair and opened it. The lights shone on her face, revealing a lady desperate to find answers. On the web, she typed, 'sources of stem cells'.

An overwhelming number of results showed up on the screen. But nearly 80% of them said the same thing: embryonic tissues, fetal tissues, adult tissues, and differentiated somatic cells. After they had been genetically reprogrammed, they were called induced pluripotent stem cells.

Jasmine's eyes rested on the embryonic and fetal tissues. It suddenly seemed as though she had cobwebs in her head. But she knew there was a reason she kept looking at these particular sources. That thought she wanted to have kept eluding her. It was there, right inside her head. But she just couldn't place it.

Having bullied her brain to recall, it finally began to fall in. But first, she searched for the sources of the first two tissues. The results revealed that they could be found in fetuses and embryos 3 to 5 days old. They could also be found in newborn babies, but not as much as in embryos.

With her fingers across her upper jaw, she gazed at the screen. Stem cells could be reprogrammed to make any kind of cell. Newborn babies were snatched from the clinic weeks after two top medical scientists were abducted. Were they all connected? Michael was a top scientist as well. Could he then be working for the same person? And was this person trying to raise an army of their own? Perhaps, with the expertise of scientists, we can modify stem cells to create superhumans.

Jasmine opened the doors, and questions saturated her head. She was convinced Michael knew something about the missing babies. How could he? He had gone from the loving man she married to a monster. Was this the experiment he had been telling her about?

She slammed the laptop shut and buried her face in her palms. Behind her chest, an irregular rhythm jammed against the walls. She sniffed deeply and pushed her hands up her forehead and across her hair. She grabbed a handful of it, putting her face down.

She raised her head after a while, breathing through pouted lips, cheeks inflating. She swished a finger across her nose and then pulled on the drawer. Tablets of Pantorex were cluttered in the small bottle as she took them.

She opened it and threw a white tablet the size of a button into her mouth. Her neck muscles glided up and down as she swallowed.

She took another deep breath and stood up. Her legs were as heavy as her heart. It seemed like she would need an Uber to the bed. But she shuffled forward and dropped her weight on it. Her hair and breasts bounced on impact. After a moment, she laid on her back. And as her eyes found the rest they had longed for all this time, her mind replayed the footage she dreaded in quick successions:

Electrohydrodynamic pump whirring – laughter echoing in the background – metal clanging – heavy breathing – footsteps shuffling – voices echoing:

"I did it, Dad! I did it!

"That's amazing, honey!"

"You've made us proud, my dear."

"Here, let me show you!"

Plug points – electric socket – machine vibrating – electricity buzzing – lights flickering:

"Turn it off!"

Electricity buzzing louder – frantic movements.

"JASMINE, TURN IT OFF!"

"I'M TRYING!"

Lights flickering – explosions – flashes of electricity discharging – electrohydrodynamic pump shuddering and then exploding – bolts of electrical discharge:

"MUM!"

"HONEY!"

Footsteps shuffling:

"No, Dad, wait!"

Electrical discharge – a light thud echoing across the room:

"DAD!"

Panic-stricken voice resounding – heavy breathing – explosions – bolts of electrical discharge – a scream – electrical buzzing – a thud – more explosions – Jasmine's body lay on the floor, unconscious.

But then a tiny voice called repeatedly in the background. Jasmine could feel the touch on her thigh. And it all began to fade.

Jasmine snapped out of her dream with one more tap of that tiny hand.

Her eyes were as though she had seen a ghost – wild and scared. And as they got acquainted with reality, they fell on little Audrey standing next to his mother and calling.

Jasmine took a deep breath and titivated her hair. "Yes, honey, mummy is here. What is it?" Her voice quivered as she spoke.

She pulled Audrey onto her bosom and cuddled him. But he did not say anything else. He just melted in her hands as she rubbed down on his hair.

Jasmine herself was trying to achieve regular breathing. Her heart hammered against the walls of her chest as she stared at the door. Flashes of memories she had tried to bury within her began to resurface – the electrical discharge hitting her mother squarely in the chest. If only her father hadn't gone for her immediately, he might still have been alive.

All that memory was starting to turn up again too deep. Droplets of sweat scattered on her forehead. But Jasmine shook her head and snapped out of it. Her throat was as though she had just completed an intra-city marathon. She swallowed hard. But that was not enough.

She looked down at Audrey, who had almost dozed off in her arms. "Come on, honey, get on the bed."

She helped him up. And as he lay comfortably, she covered him with the blanket. She stared at him with affection in her eyes as he dozed off. She kissed his forehead and then glided down the bed.

As she shoved her feet through her flip-flop, she noticed something around her ankle - blood. Her face went pale with surprise. She quickly bent low and pulled up her pajamas.

Her brows wrinkled as she found the spot the blood had trailed from. But it was not clear enough. She took her phone from the table and put on the flashlight. Rubbing off the tiny glob of congealed blood on the surface revealed a needle-point spot. It was indeed like it had been pierced with a needle, or maybe not. Maybe she had hit it on the bed dock while she was sleeping because somehow, she knew she was tossing about it all while she had that dream. But if that was the case, then there should be a swelling around the spot. In this case, there was none.

Jasmine looked around the room. Her eyes settled on her boy once again. He couldn't have hurt her. The only logical explanation was that she hit her leg on the dock while tossing about the bed. With that, she shuffled off to the kitchen for some water.

FOWLER'S ASSISTANT

Jasmine and Clark talked in her car. She called him last night and requested they meet at Pine Garden. It was an expanse of space bordered by whistling pine trees. And as the whistles traveled with the wind, the conversation grew deep.

"I feel someone's trying to take over my life – an alter ego of some sort," Jasmine told him – hands on the steering wheel.

Clark gazed at her, concern gleaming in his hazel eyes. "How do you mean?"

"They attack people and frame me up for it. They send letters, threatening me and my family. They even pick up my children from school. Although they don't harm them, I fear they might someday."

Clark adjusted his bottom on the chair to face her. "And what is your husband doing about it?"

"He doesn't know about it, and I don't want him to. He'll end up igniting everything."

"Did you, by any chance, step on the wrong toe? 'Cause I feel you must have had an encounter with the wrong people who control the city."

"You know how it is with this superhero thing: you save the day but end up on the wrong side of the same people who initiated the problem."

Clark nodded in affirmation and exhaled. "So, how do you intend to handle this person?"

"I don't know." Jasmine tapped on the steering wheel again. "That's why I called you. I wish I could deal with it once and for all before it consumes my husband or any of my kids."

An idea darted far off in Clark's head. He stared through the windshield, trying to piece it together. He glanced at Jasmine. She looked scared and already sated with the violence that was about to erupt. "I think I got an idea."

She looked at him. "What is it?"

"I think you should reach her and ask her what she wants. I'm sure she will tell you."

Jasmine stared blankly at the dashboard, processing Clark's idea. She nodded after a moment. "I think that's a good idea. Knowing what she wants will give me a head-start toward resolving the problem and getting her off my back."

"You got that right. It doesn't have to involve killing anyone."

"Yeah." Jasmine nodded. "Wait," her brows knitted, "how did you know it's a woman?"

"Just a guess," Clark shrugged. "And you know this thing called jealousy – women got it more."

"So you think framing me for crimes I didn't commit and threatening my family and me are a result of jealousy?"

"It's possible."

"That's absurd!"

"We can't rule out anything at the moment. It could be anyone. Let's not get disappointed when we see a woman instead of a man. We should be ready for anything."

Jasmine rubbed her hand up and down on the wheel. "I think you have a point."

"I do. And I think you should stop the superhero duties for now. Let's find out what the person wants first…"

Jasmine did not say a word but merely glanced at him. It would be difficult to turn a blind eye to anything that threatened the peace of her city. Clark had a point, nonetheless. She thought keeping a low profile for now was not a bad idea. Perhaps she had to tone down on how often she operated.

She was more comfortable sharing the problems that came with her superhero duties with her brother than with her therapist. She trusted him more, and he had proven to be a close confidant so far.

After their meeting, Jasmine drove toward her house. Her mind conceded flashes of thoughts: her husband's involvement with the missing infants, the needle-point injury she could not convincingly explain how it came about, and Dr. Fowler.

She drove past an Italian restaurant and made a sharp turn to the right, past the city's High Court. She was distracted for a moment, but her thoughts flowed back in a moment later.

She dwelt on the last thought as it would not leave her with a heavy mind thereafter. She hadn't set her eyes on Dr. Fowler since the night she rescued him. He may have informed her about the abduction at the clinic, but she wanted to see him. Just to be sure he was alive.

While pondering the idea, her eyes flicked at the fun shop by the road. Standing next to it were her friend, Susan, and a slender-looking man, Kyle.

He was Dr. Fowler's laboratory assistant at the time he was working on her case. She hated him at first sight. And she thought he felt the same way about her. They had no ugly incident to back up their hatred toward each other. It was always about respecting and carrying out Dr. Fowler's instructions. Besides that, there was no kind of friendship between them. This was mostly because Jasmine feared he couldn't keep her secret. But Dr. Fowler trusted him so much that he had him evaluate her sometimes. However, due to some psychological problems, as Dr. Fowler said, Kyle was dismissed from the research team 2 years after she was discharged.

Her hatred for him had faded – after all, it had no foundation. But she feared her secret identity hung on the loose now that he no longer worked with Dr. Fowler.

She had slowed down upon seeing him and Susan. They appeared to be in some deep conversation. Susan did not notice her car even when she was facing the road. Anxiety slowly crawled back up Jasmine's guts, along with that hatred she had for Kyle.

* * *

The clouds shifted, and the sun hid behind them. A halcyon wind graced the atmosphere. It was one of those normal nights—quiet, peaceful, and restful. But for some, it was not entirely peaceful.

A report about some technological advancement was being produced. However, the channel was currently running ads, so Kyle thought it was his best chance to grab that cup of popcorn he'd been craving.

He got up from the couch and shoved his feet through a pair of flip-flops. He adjusted his glasses, which had gone askew due to his position on the chair. Pulling his pajamas up his waist, he shuffled off to the kitchen. He was so slim it seemed like he would snap in two at any moment. But aside from his psychological problem, he was one research genius. For nearly a decade, he worked as Dr. Fowler's assistant, rendering his expertise in medical science.

He returned to the living room in a minute. But then he suddenly stopped in his tracks, staring at the lady standing behind the couch opposite the one he had been lying on.

"Who are you, and how did you get in here?" he questioned, keeping a calm disposition.

"It is a secret you swore to take to your grave. I didn't like you then. I don't like you now. For the promise you made to Dr. Fowler, I hope you have kept your mouth shut."

"I may suffer from dementia, but I can never forget that voice. I can never forget that annoying aura of courage and dominance that was being thrown in my face every day some years ago."

"I'm glad you remember. Recent events have made me wonder if you are still loyal to the promise you made. Somehow, it seems like someone has been busy singing my true identity to my enemies. I wanted to be sure it wasn't you."

Kyle shuffled to the chair and sat down, adjusting his glasses. "My loyalty is to Dr. Fowler. I owe him that for how good he's been to me. And whatever promise I made to him, I shall keep till my last breath. If it were to you, I'd been singing not only to your enemies but to the police."

Those last words struck a nerve. Azra glared hard at him. She wouldn't deny for a moment she felt like strangling him to death. How they felt about each other clearly hadn't changed over the years.

"I sincerely hope for your sake you keep to your promise no matter what."

She opened the door and stormed outside, slamming it shut behind her. Kyle casually set his eyes back on the TV that had continued to play in the background all the while.

"Erm, Azra, I think there's something going on at Dr. Fowler's house," Zuri reported.

Azra stopped in her tracks, finger on the intercom. "What is it?"

"I'm seeing some unusual movements around the house. I think he's under attack."

"What?"

Azra skipped toward her bike, which was parked a stone's throw away. "Is Dr. Fowler on sight?"

"No."

"Keep a close watch on the house. I'm on my way."

Dr. Fowler's residence was a few kilometers away. It was another race against time. Azra mounted her bike and fired the engine. Tires screeched against the tarmac as she turned in a C manner and zoomed off, the front tires lifting off and bouncing back on the ground.

She dashed out of the street, down another road, and through an alley. It led her out to a ring road. From here, she navigated her way to the express. She had thrown every caution to the wind at this time.

"Juli, what's going on at the house?" she inquired.

"It all seems quiet."

Azra hit the top gear and fired harder on the accelerator. Speed was no enemy of the Kawasaki Ninja. It flew in the direction of the wind and was streamlined for active turbo-charge. Azra guided her way past cars and other bikes. She was ahead of other drivers before they could even blink. All she thought about was Dr. Fowler. She feared the worst in this second attack.

In less than 5 minutes, she had covered 10km. While in motion, she turned off the bike. The lights went out, but it continued to a tree by the street's entrance. A car drove by, with its headlamps bright and revealing. But Azra had parked in an area covered by a shade almost thicker than darkness.

She stole out from behind the tree. In the cover of darkness, she wound her way to No.5 of the street. Her extra speed and her ability to blend perfectly into her environment like a chameleon gave her an added advantage.

She stood behind the tree opposite Dr. Fowler's residence for a short time. It all seemed quiet.

"What's the update, Juli?"

"Seems quiet on the inside. But you gotta be careful."

"Why?"

"I can only tell what falls within the camera perimeter, but I don't think those guys came to his house just to look around…"

"You mean they're no longer in there?"

"I don't think so."

Azra watched the house closely from her lair. It appeared quiet indeed. Dr. Fowler could be sleeping already. She would have seen his shadow behind the glowing white curtains if not. But again, if he were asleep, the lights would be switched off.

She scanned both ends of the street. All clear! She crossed the road. She approached the house from the left side, eyes on the windows. One can never tell what lies in wait.

One step at a time, she went closer to the door. Her movements aligned with the direction of the wind. She felt no drag on her feet. Her senses, especially of hearing, were as sharp as those of an Impala's. She did not think she had any need for her gun yet – after all, she could still capture the men without them.

Her eyes scanned the surroundings like those of a trained assassin. Like a cat prowling, her muscles were ready to spring into action at the slightest agitation.

Another cautious step brought her to the door. She looked at both sides of the building and then headed for the window. It was easy to think she was a spy or even an assassin – her costume suited the latter.

She crept up to the window and tried to look through. But the curtains were not transparent enough, and she could only see the glow in the room.

She padded back to the door and curled her fingers around the handle. It was quiet inside as she leaned her ear against the door, and she seemed clear to move in.

Turning the handle and pushing the door slightly inward, she snuck a peek inside. The sitting room seemed clear. The rest of her body filtered through.

She reached for her gun while her eyes sized up everywhere – from the shelf carrying the hourglass on one corner of the living room to the chairs and then up the stairs. It didn't seem like there was anyone in here. But her hand stayed firm on the gun.

At this point, it would have been right to announce her presence. Dr. Fowler would come downstairs. But she wanted to be sure it was safe to do that. And the fact that the door was unlocked made her suspect foul play.

She looked behind the chairs before making her way upstairs.

However, as she walked past the shelf, she heard something. She stopped in her tracks and listened. A device somewhere was giving off beeps. Instantly, her senses went on a high alert, and her anxiety heightened.

She looked for it around the shelf and behind the chairs. Her frantic movements made her stub her toes against the table. Even so, she did not find the device. And it did not stop beeping.

Azra stood still, taking deep breaths. Her chest rose and fell heavily as she let air through her mouth.

Having calmed herself, she listened again. The sound was clearer and louder this time. She traced the source to the underside of the staircase. A C4 timer was planted on the wall.

3 seconds remaining.

"Oh, Shit!"

Her muscles activated a quick flight response. She dashed to the door and threw herself out. She landed just beyond the three flights of stairs outside. But she quickly got back on her feet and dived farther away. At the same time, the bungalow exploded, throwing her even farther.

Azra crashed to the ground and grabbed a handful of sand and grass, letting out a groan. She was injured. But with muscles taut and a deep grimace on her face, she scrambled back. A shower of shards and splinters rained on the ground like snow as more of the building exploded. An inferno rose to the once-peaceful skies, carrying with it dark clouds of smoke.

"Azra, are you okay?" Zuri inquired.

But she did not answer. She was struggling to get on her feet. But her hands shook, not able to provide the strength she needed. Her eyes had gone droopy, and her vision blurry. She yelped as she put in another effort. A police siren blared somewhere in the distance. Trouble! She would be arrested if they met her here.

She groaned aloud as she made another attempt at getting on her feet. The part of her pants covering her left calf had soaked with blood. Her back seemed injured as well.

"Azra, talk to me – are you okay?"

"No, I think…"

"It's okay. Stay where you are. I'm coming to get you."

"Don't worry, I'll be fine.

"But you're hurt."

"Stay back, Zuri, I'll be fine!"

That was an order, and Zuri wasn't going to flout it. But she herself was overwhelmed with anxiety.

Azra tried once again. This time, she applied every ounce of strength left in her, yelling all the while. Finally, she managed to get herself on her feet, limping. But her knees buckled, unable to carry her weight. Migraine seared through her head, with her surroundings squeezing and splicing.

She fell back but did reach the ground. Two hands caught her in mid-air. She turned to check out the face of the person who had caught her. But her eyes were half-closed. And in a moment, they fell shut.

The man lifted her onto his shoulder and thumped down the street, her arms dangling behind him all the while. The police were close, as announced by their sirens. Zuri had been calling on Azra all the while.

The man spotted Azra's bike behind the sycamore tree. Although it didn't have 'Azra' inscribed on it, he knew it was hers somehow.

He went for it. And as quickly as he could, he made Azra lean on him in front. The bike was automatic. He clearly knew how to work it, for he easily located the button.

The engine soon shut to life. The man hit the gear and rode off. Dr. Fowler's residence, with him inside, was in ruins, crackling like burning trees.

FRIEND AND ALLY

Azra lay on her back on a bunk bed. Her jacket had been removed, leaving the chest binder around her. Below the binder were strips of bandages running the circumference of her body. The man had treated her.

He could have removed her pants as well. But he had great respect for her. So, he had cut off the parts covering her left calf. And having treated it, he had bandaged it as well.

And now, he sat next to the bed, staring at her. He hadn't removed the mask, but he seemed to recognize her. He had only unplugged the intercom as Zuri wouldn't stop calling on Azra, and he didn't bother to answer.

Azra moved her fingers and then her head. The man sat still, watching. She tilted her head again. Slowly, she opened her eyes. It was all blurry at first, but her eyes got acquainted with her environment after a while.

The roof was made of thick, unpolished timber. The wall on her left was the same as the roof. But as she turned to her right, she saw the man. In shock, she tried to clamber to a sitting position. But a sharp pain seared through her back, reaching her head. She yelped and placed her hand on her chest.

At the same time, the man rushed in and held her shoulders. "Lie still; you're not strong enough yet."

But Azra stared at him, face pale with shock. "Sylvester?"

"Jo!"

Azra tried to get back up again. This time, he helped her sit on the bed, her feet touching the ground. She groaned all the while.

"How did you find me?" she asked, staring at him as though she had been running from him all her life.

But Sylvester quickly corrected that:

"For the record, I was never looking for you. I was walking by the road when I saw a house on fire. I ran to it and saw you wounded. I've pretty much heard about a lady that goes about beating up the bad guys. She wears a mask and calls herself 'Azra' (making the quotation sign). So when I saw you, I had to help. I only recognized it was Jasmine, the girl that turned me down at high school when I was treating you."

"You took off my mask?" Azra's eyes widened.

"I didn't have to." He rubbed his hands together like he actually did.

Azra looked at the bandages across her belly. She didn't seem bothered about Sylvester seeing her chest binder. Then her eyes went down her calf. It was not bright enough in the cabin, but she could see the bandages.

She looked up at him. "Thank you."

"It was nothing. Just get enough rest, and you'll be fine. The injuries aren't deep."

Azra nodded and glanced around the cabin. It was a bit clumsy in here: from the couch to the small refrigerator, to the wooden cloth hanger just above a pile of books, to the rack next to it. Sylvester himself sat next to the table. There couldn't be proper ventilation in the cabin, Azra thought – although it felt cool at the moment and had a minty smell.

"So, what are you doing here?" she questioned, still glancing around.

"This is my house."

"What? You live here?" Her brows furrowed.

"Not good enough?"

"No, not what I mean. It's just…"

"I wanted a quiet place," Sylvester cut in. "After all the shit in the military, I wanted somewhere quiet, away from people."

Azra nodded submissively. It didn't seem like she had a choice after all. She had taken note of the man she was sitting with while he talked. Although he had the same light-brown cat eyes and full, jet-black hair, he seemed different from the shy introvert she had known back in high school. One of the reasons she turned him down when he finally managed to summon the courage to tell her about his feelings was his lack of confidence. Now, he appeared to have more confidence around his shoulders than she had seen in any man.

"Yeah, I heard you left for the military after high school. What happened?"

"I'm sorry, but I don't wanna talk about it."

"It's okay."

She removed her mask and tucked her hair behind her ear.

"What about you? I wouldn't believe if I was told that in years to come, the beautiful Jasmine Hanson would be playing superhero duties for Wonder City instead of working in a big industry and inventing stuff."

She gave a sideways smile. "It's a long story."

"Yeah, I thought so." He exhaled deeply and rubbed his hands on his pants. "And you should check out your intercom. Someone's been calling."

Upon hearing that, Azra recoiled. Reality struck her. Dr. Fowler died in the explosion. Grief took over her features like a raincloud.

"Are you okay? Did I say something wrong?" Sylvester questioned.

She sniffed in and breathed out through her mouth. "The man in the house that exploded helped me when my parents died. And now, I couldn't save him."

She bent low and covered her face with her arms, sobbing. Sylvester moved over and sat on the bed. He took her hand and massaged it gently.

"Hey, it wasn't your fault. You tried to save him. It was too late, unfortunately. Don't put the blame on yourself. It'll weigh you down. Not good for the fight ahead."

He draped his hand across her shoulders. She sniffed deeply again and looked up. Her eyes had turned bloodshot and teary.

"Don't be so hard on yourself, Jo. I've seen what it can do to people. Get a hold of your emotions and march on. That's what soldiers do. I'm sure Dr. Fowler knows it wasn't your fault."

He rubbed down on her arm. Those feelings of love he had buried years ago tingled his body. But he pushed them aside at once.

And as though Azra knew what was going on inside of him, she wrapped up her emotions with another deep breath.

"Thank you. I'm fine," she nodded, voice quivering.

Sylvester left her and returned to his chair.

"What's the time?" she asked.

"There!" He pointed at the clock hung on the wall.

Azra looked. It was 3:25 pm. Too late to go home. But she could return to the base.

"Please give me that." She pointed at the intercom on the table.

Sylvester handed it to her. She plugged it in at once.

"Zuri, are you there?"

"Oh my goodness! Azra, are you okay? You got me worried!"

"I'm fine. I'll be at the base in a few minutes."

"Okay."

"In a few minutes?" Sylvester cut in. "You're not fit enough yet to ride."

"I was thinking you'd take me there."

"What?"

"Yeah. I'd like you to join us."

"Nah," Sylvester shook his head. "I'm not ready for all that violence. I just want peace and quiet."

"It doesn't stop you from enjoying your peace and quiet. Besides, we only operate at night."

"I'm sorry, Jo, but I can't. I've been out of the field for nearly 2 years now. I don't intend to go back anytime soon."

Azra realized he wasn't going to agree immediately. She would have to give him some time.

"I urge you to think about it. I'll be stopping by from time to time to know if you've changed your mind."

Sylvester did not say another word. The bed creaked as Azra released her weight on it, trying to get her feet back on the ground. Sylvester moved in and helped her.

"You gonna take me to the camp or what?" she asked.

He glanced at her. She seemed to have forgotten that she had turned him down and was no longer allowed to use that commanding tone of voice on him, but he let it slide anyway.

"I will," he replied.

Azra didn't think he would betray her. She trusted that he would not give away her location. And so she was willing to take him to the base even when he declined her offer.

* * *

Jasmine returned home at 5 a.m. She told her husband that she and her brother, Clark, had a lot of catching up to do, and it lasted the whole night. She was uncomfortable lying to him in this manner, but she had no choice.

She came through the roof opening with a lot of effort. She muffled the groans and yelps until her feet touched the floor.

Already changed to her pajamas in the base, she limped straight to her kids' room. They were still sleeping.

She came and stood by the bed, staring at them as they both cuddled on their teddies. She knew she was failing in her duties as a mother. She hadn't been there for them. She might have put them to bed herself last night, but they were being denied her protection, her attention. Putting them to bed was definitely not enough. She hoped to deal with her alter ego and get back to being the amazing mother she had always been.

She padded to her room, hoping to find her husband on the bed. But as she opened the door, she discovered he wasn't there. The bed looked like it hadn't been slept on through the night.

It was to her advantage – at least she didn't have to lie to him anymore. But that meant Melissa and Audrey slept all alone in the house.

She dropped her weight on the bed, her hair bouncing along. She rubbed her hands like a remorseful child. Her chest thumped with guilt. It was unfair for her children, she thought. The more she tried to balance her nightlife and being a mother, the farther she drifted toward the former. There had to be a way.

She looked around the room. Her guilt still hounded her. As much as she needed a good rest, being in her children's room would lighten her emotions.

She stood up and returned to the kids' room. She took the chair and sat down next to the bed, watching them as they slept.

After about 20 minutes, sleep began to creep in. She nodded the air as she tried to stay away. She could have easily gone to her room to sleep. But she wanted to put herself through the torture as a way of paying penance for abandoning her children throughout the night. And she may not be considering that, but her kids would be up by 7 and then come to her room. It was pointless sleeping for only an hour.

The head-butting and swaying continued until 6:20 am when the front door creaked open. Michael was back. The sound of the door woke Jasmine up. Now that the children were still asleep, she thought it was the best time to confront him about the note.

She stood up and marched out of the room. Michael had his briefcase in one hand and his coat in the other hand, making his way up the stairs when Jasmine stepped out.

"Good morning, honey," he greeted.

That greeting lightened the look on Jasmine's face. "Good morning, honey," she responded rather forcefully, standing by the top flight stairs.

Michael got to where she was and kissed her on the cheek. He pulled back and sized her up, noticing how exhausted she looked. "You don't seem all right, honey. Something wrong?"

Jasmine frowned as if she had caught him cheating on her. But she took his briefcase from him nonetheless. "We need to talk," she told him, making for their room.

Michael gazed at her. With his droopy eyes, he seemed to need a good dose of sleep. He removed his tie and followed her.

"What do you know about the missing babies?" she asked immediately, and the door banged shut behind him.

"What are you talking about? What babies?" Michael put on his coat and knotted his tie on the bed like one getting ready for a fight.

"The infants abducted from New Haven Clinic."

"I don't know what you're talking about."

"Don't play dumb with me, Michael; you know what I'm talking about." Her voice was getting louder and fiercer now, although she hadn't realized it yet.

"I got no idea what you're talking about. What could I possibly know about some missing babies? I'm not a detective, for goodness sake." He went to the bed and snatched his coat and tie, storming toward the wardrobe.

"Then why is there a note in your pocket saying, 'keep the stem cells alive'?"

Michael halted his movements. He had turned red in the nose. He gripped his shirt so tight it threatened to rip apart. "You now snoop around my things when I'm not around?"

"That's not the point. Just answer the question!" Jasmine herself had gone scarlet in the face, ready for the fight that was about to break out.

"Well, if you must know, it was a note from the chief scientist about the stem cells we grew in the lab. It has nothing to do with the missing babies."

Jasmine stepped closer, clenching her fist. "How pathetic you are at lying, Michael. If the note was all about the stem cells you grew in your lab, why did you hide the paper immediately when you saw me enter the room that day?"

Michael did not seem to have the right answer for that. She glared at Jasmine with foaming lips and bulging eyes.

"ANSWER ME!" she demanded.

"I've got nothing else to say to you." He went to the closet and began to hang his coat.

"Yeah." Jasmine nodded. "I know that's how this is gonna play out. But I'm gonna investigate and…"

Her phone chimed on the table. She stopped talking for a moment and looked. It was Zuri.

She picked up the phone and slid her thumb across it.

"Yeah?"

Michael might look like he was minding his business, but his ears were in the conversation.

"What?" Jasmine blared.

The call ended. Jasmine looked at Michael briefly and then stormed out of the room. She descended the stairs to the sitting room and put on the TV.

A report was going on. On the left side of the TV was a photo of Azra at

Dr. Fowler's door before the explosion. Beneath the photo was the tag, 'Azra WANTED.'

Shock smoldered up Jasmine's face like smoke from clumps of sawdust. Someone was taking a photo of her all the while she was trying to get into Dr. Fowler's residence. The hand holding the remote shook with fervor. It was hard to believe. How could she be so careless?

She turned up the volume of the TV, glancing up at the staircase. She didn't want her husband to see her expressing emotions over a report that shouldn't concern her.

"…the police have already begun a manhunt for the self-acclaimed super-hero. They believe that in due time, they will apprehend her. Recall that the abduction at New Haven Clinic was also linked to her. The case is still under investigation. However, the lady's actions leave people wondering what her true intentions are. Whoever has information on her whereabouts is required by law to report to the nearest precinct…"

Jasmine turned down the volume. She'd had enough. It appears she had finally landed herself into trouble. Whoever planted that bomb obviously knew she would come there. But how they knew was what baffled her. Whatever she did, they seemed to be two steps ahead. They kept setting traps to drag her deeper into the mud, and she kept falling into it. Another attack, and she was being framed for it.

She stared at her photo on the TV screen. It was the moment she had turned toward the window. It was imperative that she clear her name; otherwise, not only would Azra's good image be permanently destroyed, but she would also have to stop being a superhero.

THE OPERATION

Azra and Sylvester stood at the analytical screen half the size of a snooker table. The screen displayed Amalex Limited's digital blueprint. Jasmine slid her hand across the screen to position it perfectly, as it was in 3D format.

"This is it?" Sylvester asked.

"Yeah," she answered.

He glanced from one end of the screen to another. Different sections of a large complex. "How sure are you about this information?"

"Very sure," Zuri cut in, swiveling around and facing them. "Let me tell you: this guy has been asking me out on a date for a long time. But I've always turned him down. However, 4 days ago, I needed to get out and have fun. So when he came around and made the same request, I agreed. While on the date, we talked about a lot of things, including work. He told me he was a laboratory scientist. He trusted me enough to tell me that his institute was working on a project. He didn't say what the project was all about, though. He only said it was life-changing. But he said there was something missing in the project…"

"What was that?"

"Xyline."

Sylvester's face puckered with confusion. "What's that?"

"A chemical. He said it was necessary for the completion of the project. However, the company involved said they wouldn't sell it without an express order from the minister of science and research. He told me they had the best scientists working on this particular project. I pieced his words together like solving a puzzle and came to the conclusion that he was working for the same person who had been fighting against Azra. I also researched and discovered that the chemical could be bought from one source only: Amalex Limited."

"Hmm…" Sylvester scratched his chin. "So, how did you learn about the operation?"

"We went out yesterday. And while he was showing me some photos on his phone, a message came in. It read: 'Op X, 11:57 pm, tomorrow night'. He swiped off the message almost instantly. And that cultivated a thought in me. Having worked as a decryptor for years, it was easy to decode messages like that…"

"Yeah, it's clear enough: Operation Xyline…"

"You got that!"

Sylvester returned his gaze to the screen with his hands on his waist.

"It's the reason I had Juli extract the blueprint of the Amalex complex, so we can map out a strategy for a counterattack," Azra spoke, looking at the screen.

Zuri swiveled back to her screen.

"It's a large complex, but we don't have to go through every part of it, yeah?" Sylvester intoned.

"Of course not. We believe the chemical will be in either of two places: the repository or the storage. The operation is expected to be carried out in these places. So, must be ready."

"I see this is the repository." Sylvester pointed.

"Yes. Next to it is the manufacturing department. I hope the operation does not alert the workers there…"

"But you know that's almost impossible, right? There's no way an attack and a counterattack will be going on in the repository, and the workers in the manufacturing department won't know about it."

"You're right. If it were possible to keep counter discreetly…"

"And you think those attacking will handle it the same way?"

Azra dropped her shoulders, along with a breath. "We'll take on whatever happens then. And here," she pointed, "is the storage. My instincts tell me this is where the chemical will be. So, this is where the operation will likely take place."

Sylvester nodded again, white light reflecting on his face. "What about the entrances and the exit points? Are there emergency exits? The security around these areas...?"

Azra made sure to clear the air before the time. It was a chance to get back at whoever had been fighting her. She did not want to mess things up. It was for this reason that she had solicited Sylvester's help.

She had kept a low profile for one week. That had given her the chance to make amends with her family. She took her kids to school and brought them back herself. No hitches. She played with them. No unusual disappearances. She was at home most of the time, only breezing in and out of the base some nights. She had kept a close watch on her husband. But as though he knew, he had kept a clean profile. Two nights ago, they had made up and made love. Once again, she had enjoyed the bliss of a peaceful home, her wounds healing throughout the time.

And when Zuri presented this opportunity, she was willing to oblige her. She had traced her way to Sylvester's cabin and had spent a lot of time convincing him to join her in the operation.

"Just this one," he had noted.

"Yes, just this one."

And now, they both suited up, having understood their assignment. Azra was in her usual costume.

"Still looking forward to wearing the new costume," she told Zuri as she tucked a pistol down its holster

"I'm still working on it. Trust me, it's gonna be one of a kind."

Sylvester had no need for a special costume. He was not one of them, after all. It was all casual to him: black combat jeans and a gray body-hugging long-sleeve shirt, revealing his brawny physique even more. Tucked down his waist were different caliber pistols of the Glock model. A Barret M82A1 was locked and loaded in his hand, making him look military.

"What's the time?" Azra asked.

"11:05 pm," Zuri answered, rolling backward and getting up from the chair.

"We should get going." She marched toward the bike.

"Sylvester," Zuri called. He looked. "Here."

She handed him an intercom.

"Oh…" he cocked a brow and plugged it in.

"Make sure you come back here alive, both of you," she warned.

"We'll try…"

The Kawasaki Ninja cruised out to the open. Azra was the rider. Zuri had provided them with safety helmets. Sylvester sat comfortably as Azra took him on a ride.

"You sure you're good at this?" he asked.

"Fasten your seatbelt."

They covered the 2km through Regent Base in less than 2 minutes. In no time, the Kawasaki Ninja was on the road. Amalex Limited was only 5km due north. It was a free industry by way. They would only encounter trucks and vans on the way.

Azra powered the engine, bringing the Ninja's usual speed to life. The Ninja blazed at more than 60mph. Sylvester had to squint as the wind threatened to blow his eyes out.

And when they entered the byway, the bike easily swayed past trucks and vans. Azra was clearly enjoying the bends and turns. For Sylvester, not so much.

"Careful!" he warned at the top of his voice. Only out of manliness had he not wrapped his arms around her.

But having sighted the green light at the peak of the Amalex complex, she slowed down.

"What time is it?"

"11:16," Sylvester answered.

"Juli, any unusual?"

"None yet. All clear!"

Azra was almost a hundred meters away from the complex. Now, she looked for a safe spot to park.

"Remind me: how far is the repository from the storage?" Sylvester inquired.

"Just 2 blocks away. I'm parking between those two trucks." She pointed.

They were barely 50 meters away from the complex at this point. The two trucks were parked in reserve within the premises to serve as cover for the bike. Azra switched off the lights and rode between them.

Having secured the bike, Azra and Sylvester thumped toward the complex.

It was a large industry covering several acres of space, about the size of a mega football stadium. Trucks and vans, most likely for delivery purposes, were parked around the premises. As they approached the complex, its name became clear on the boards across the center building. It glowed green, with a golden oil drop beside it as its logo.

The complex and its surroundings shone with white lights, as illuminated as a surgeon's theater. The shades cast by the trucks and vans were the only means through which the superheroes could reach the intended departments without being noticed.

"It's too bright here," Sylvester commented, hiding behind a truck.

"Yeah, and I think I got an idea of the mode of operation for the thieves."

"Turn off the lights?"

"Exactly!"

"I thought so, too."

"That's the only way they can reach the repository or the storage without being spotted by the security cameras."

Sylvester looked toward the name board. A CCTV hung next to it. That was just one of many, he thought.

"Do you think we can still find our way to the repository and the storage if the lights go out?" he asked.

"Yes, but we don't have to wait until it happens. We have to get closer." She looked at her watch. It was 11:25 p.m. We still have time to make our observations while we wait for the operation."

Sylvester poked his head out from behind the truck. He scanned the area.

"Worry not, guys," Zuri spoke. "I've been able to hack into the security system. I'll turn the cameras away for every department you get to so they don't detect your presence."

"Good job, girl," Azra commended.

"Make no mistake about it: the whole place is studded with security cameras. It would have been almost impossible to bypass them all without being seen."

"Now you're showing off," Sylvester teased.

"You jealous?" she giggled.

"I don't have to. I'm not pretty techy myself."

"I'll make out to teach you for just a few dollars."

"You wish."

"Get on with it, Juli, we don't have much time," Azra cut in.

"On it." After a moment, she reported, "Done!"

Sylvester poked his head out again and looked at the camera. It had turned in the opposite direction.

"Let's go."

But even though the cameras had been turned off, they still had to be wary of human eyes. No one was on the front part of the complex, but those inside could still see them.

Cautiously, they moved from one truck to another, keeping their presence away from the lights. Their boots crunched against the sand. That would have betrayed them to anyone close by.

Not long enough, they got to the last truck. From this point to the walkway, there were no shades. Although Zuri would turn the cameras, they stood at high risk of being spotted. Anyone who did would raise an alarm at once, not with that M82 hanging down Sylvester's neck.

"What do we do now?" he asked.

"Juli, the cams?" Azra inquired.

"Turned away."

She looked around the walkway. There was, unfortunately, nowhere they could take cover.

"I think we…"

And just like Azra had said, the lights went out, and the whole Amalex complex was in total darkness.

"I think they're here. Come on."

The heroes stomped toward the repository, Azra leading the way.

"But that's earlier than they had planned," Zuri spoke.

"What happened to the element of surprise?" Sylvester replied.

He and Azra hurried down the walkway, with the gun bouncing off his chest and being careful not to be seen.

At the end, the walkway split into two: one to the left and the other to the right.

"Which way now?" Sylvester asked.

Azra looked left and right. "This way," she pointed to the right. She was supposed to have the map in her head. Any wrong turn could jeopardize their efforts. Zuri was there to direct the way should they get lost, nonetheless. But getting lost was not an option at the moment.

They navigated from one walkway to another, yet they did not encounter any of the workers. Zuri did not have to bother about turning the cameras away, as the whole place was dark.

Sylvester stopped for a moment and removed his rifle. He forced it up his shirt in a bid to hide it. It may not have been perfectly concealed, but it was away from direct sight.

They arrived at the marketing department as inscribed on the board across the block. Workers shuffled about with their phone's flashlights showing the way. But as the heroes zipped past the doorway, a security guard sitting by the door spotted them:

"Hey, stop right there!"

They were forced to halt their movements. He took apprehensive steps toward them – his right hand wrapped around the handle and the left supporting it at the base. As he walked closer, he took out his flashlight. But Azra wasn't going to let that happen.

Before he flipped the switch, she strode across the walkway and struck his neck with the side of her palm. He faded. She caught him. Sylvester moved in.

"How the hell did you do that?" he asked as he took one of the guard's arms.

"That's not important now. Come on."

Together, they dragged the man's body into an embrasure along the walkway.

OPERATION II

Sylvester poked his head out of the embrasure. He saw a worker make a cross to the other side of the block, and now it was all clear. "Come on."

Azra led the way. She had not told him about her superpowers yet. And seeing her move that fast left him some questions, some of which he already had an answer to. He thought she was under the influence of some kind of speed-enhancing drugs.

More workers were starting to plod the walkway, and that meant more eyes on the two strange people in their midst. The manufacturing department was about 3 blocks away. For Sylvester, it was the gun protruding off of his shirt – for Azra, it was her mask. And now they both had to remain in the cover of darkness as more flashlights were coming on.

They soon broke off with a run. Through the Packaging block, they turned to the walkway leading to the inspection block. They skipped down the walkway and veered through another down the right. Luckily, they hadn't been spotted by another guard who would have seen the shape of the Barret behind Sylvester's shirt.

The whirring and churning of machines announced their closeness to the manufacturing department. It was the largest block, stretching several meters across. Big and small pipes, like in a refinery, ran end to end, branching off at different points. Vats as big as fractionating towers stood, with pipes like those in an oil rig running into and out of them. Greeted with a stale smell, Azra pinched her nose. But Sylvester seemed to be used to smells like this.

There were only a few workers out here with their flashlights on. But the heroes found a way to evade them.

Azra pointed at the passageway leading to the repository. It split through the manufacturing block like a tunnel. Workers were crossing the passageway, but only one or two of them had their flashlights on. Azra and Sylvester ran past them. They might have noticed something, for some of them looked back. It was, however, too dark to tell what they looked like.

The repository was notched to the left, nearly half the size of the manufacturing block. The dull green light revealed the 'Amalex Repository' written across the block.

"There it is," Azra pointed, panting for breath.

They stood behind the pillar facing the block. Bottles clinked, and racks clattered ceremoniously inside. Workers traversed the walkway, oblivious to what was going on.

"Seems peaceful," Sylvester observed, looking from one end of the block to another and through the windows.

"That's the plan, Syl. Cut off the lights and take what you came for without raising an alarm."

"I'm guessing they have an insider. The lights should be back on by now."

"Depends on the extent of the damage in the powerhouse. Here's what we're going to do: you'll stay here and keep a close watch while I go to the Storage. I'll let you know if I see anything – you, likewise."

"I don't think this is the place, but it's okay. Go ahead."

Azra scuttled away. Sylvester would have to find a better cover – maybe get a little closer to the block.

Azra skipped down the walkway. It appeared Sylvester had been slowing her down, for she did so at a much faster pace. Her limbs carried her slim frame with ease. She steered from one walkway to another, ghosting past the workers.

She covered 3 blocks in less than 3 minutes. 'Storage' was written across the wall of the two-story block built in a square form, leaving a space at the center. All around the passageways, workers moved about, carrying racks and trolleys. Glasses clinked, and crates clattered. It was much brighter here as there were more flashlights than in any other block the heroes crossed.

Azra stood behind a pillar and observed the block and everyone she set her eyes on. She had removed her mask at this time so as not to draw any unnecessary attention to herself. Only a few workers on the lower walkway noticed her presence and unavoidably gave her that questionable look.

But there was this lady on the top floor. Azra noticed she kept stealing glances at her while pushing a trolley. It was unusual because she was dressed like every other worker in this block – a green jumpsuit with the name 'Amalex' on the left side of the chest. Azra surmised she must be up to something to have seen her from the top walkway.

Her eyes dropped on the contents of the trolley. The flashlights around the lady revealed an almost empty trolley. Azra couldn't exactly tell what was in it, but she knew there was something. The lady walked faster, stealing glances at her. Their eyes met in a common line whenever she did.

Azra stormed toward the staircase, having spotted it earlier. She kept an eye on the lady. Unfortunately, the staircase's turn blocked her off. Noticing this, the lady dashed through a door along the walkway.

Azra skipped up the stairs faster than a javelin launched into the air. But the lady was nowhere in sight by the time she got to the top floor. She scanned everywhere and everyone. And then she saw the door. It was half open. Without a second thought, she ran to it, swaying past the workers. Flashlights revealed her face, but her quick movements allowed not a glimpse.

She went through the door. It was cold here as if an air conditioner was somewhere. But it was difficult to see in the thick darkness. However, Azra noticed the downward staircase.

Azra skipped the first two flights. But as her feet touched the third, she spotted a door on her left. She quickly went for it.

She threw it open but met a host of workers chattering. As flashlights revealed, refrigerators were along the sides. Some of them turned to the lady by the door.

"Sorry," she whispered and shut it back.

The lady couldn't have gone in there, she thought. At this time, it was starting to get more suspicious. She was starting to think the lady could be the agent sent to get the chemical.

Her lissome limbs took her down the stairs. She turned sharply to the other side and coasted down in a flash.

She stormed through the door in front of her. A quick glance outside didn't reveal anything at first. But then she spotted someone cross a wall toward the lounge. It happened so fast it could have been a mirage.

Azra zipped toward the lounge. The lady was just walking through the exit when Azra got to the lounge.

"Hey!"

But the lady was out of sight. Azra ran through the door. She saw him clutching on something wrapped with a piece of cloth. That was definitely the bottle of chemicals!

"Stop!" she beckoned.

But the lady did the opposite. She ran off. Azra chased after her, turning on the jets in her muscles.

The lady sped down a walkway and branched off to another lounge. Azra arrived almost at the same time. The lady stood, ready to settle it once and for all.

"Why are you following me?" she asked.

"Hand the bottle over, and I'll let you go."

"That's not possible! And I advise you to stop following me, or you'll regret it."

She turned toward the door. But Azra whizzed forward and stood in front of her. She flung her leg toward her head, but she blocked it off with her left and punched the lady's neck with her right. It was a light touch. She staggered backward, coughing.

"I don't wanna fight you. Just hand the damn bottle over," Azra warned.

"You have to get through me first."

Azra sighed. "As you wish."

The lady laid the bottle gently on the floor and stretched her hands. Azra made a dash for the bottle, but she kicked her hand off and threw a punch at her face. Azra grabbed her fist, flung it aside, and then wrapped her arm around her neck.

She thumped to the wall, scaled through a height, and flipped backward. She could have twisted Azra's hands and taken over the chokehold. But Azra immediately turned. Her feet touched the ground, lifted her up, and threw her against the wall. Her body slammed against it and thudded on the hard, bare ground.

She looked next to her and picked up the bottle of Xyline hidden behind a piece of cloth. She turned it over and over as if to be sure it was the right bottle.

The lady got on her feet and strode toward Azra. She slid out of the way. But somehow, she broke her pace and kicked the bottle off Azra's hands. Azra gave her a kick to her belly and then went for the bottle. But the lady managed to regain her stance, pulled Azra back, and dived forward instead. She caught the bottle and dashed through the door.

Azra went after her. She crossed another walkway and made it out to what seemed like the company's backyard. There were more trucks here, huge steel pipes running from one end to another. The lady ran through the trucks toward an SUV parked some distance away.

"Hey, hold it right there!" a security guard blared, running out from one of the blocks and leveling his gun at the ladies.

But it was dangerous to fire a shot in a place overrun with pipes carrying gases and liquid chemicals. He only had to join in the race.

Azra kept a hot pursuit of the girl. Somehow, she had managed to lengthen the distance between them. Azra noticed she was heading for the car and increased her pace. At this point, her superpowers kicked in.

A few yards away from the car, the door slid open. A man sat by the door, pointing a gun in the lady's direction. But with the lady in his path, he couldn't shoot.

She hurled the bottle at the SUV as though she knew Azra was about to catch up with her. The man stumbled out to catch it. At the same time, Azra stopped in her tracks.

She took a one-time deep breath and closed her eyes. Her senses aligned with the elements. She stretched forth her hand toward the east, in the same direction as the wind. Just before the bottle landed on the man's hand, a gust of wind dragged it off. It flew across the air at top speed and dropped on Azra's hand. Her mouth fell agape. Her face turned pale as she gazed at the bottle in her hand.

Gunshots crackled in the air. Azra sped off with the bottle. The lady went after her. But Azra turned on the engines. Bullets clanked off the steel pipes as she steered through the trucks and into the block. The lady had probably lost her way, for she was nowhere behind Azra.

"Syl, meet me at the rendezvous now. Run as fast as you can," Azra ordered.

She zipped through the passageways, past the workers – some of whom screamed upon a light collision. With the gunshots, the security had been alerted. Footsteps thumped from different directions. And while the tension spread throughout the company, with more security men and workers knowing about the invasion, the lights came on. Once again, the whole of Amalex shone like a football stadium.

Azra had already put her mask back on, but even so, her identity was at risk. She slipped through the workers, who were now scampering for safety and locking up everywhere. An alarm resounded through the company, alerting every security guard.

"SHE'S HERE!" a guard called.

But he had only seen her for a moment. Before backup arrived, Azra had already coasted down the walkway and barged through a door. Not sure where she had gone, the guards went in another direction.

More footsteps stomped the ground, shaking the foundations of Amalex Limited. Azra had yet to know how far she could go in a minute. This scenario gave her a hint. Perhaps it was due to tension, but her pace had increased to 70mph. Her limbs were almost invisible in the air as they flailed nearly as fast as the blades of an electric fan. She was being carried by the wind, darting past guards and workers before they could even catch a glimpse.

In less than two minutes, she reached the rendezvous. She mounted the bike and put the bottle between her legs. Firing it on would alert the guards of her whereabouts. All she had to do was wait for Sylvester.

Having been spotted by some security men, she had cleared Sylvester's path. So it shouldn't take him too long to get to the bike. Her fingers wrapped around the handle, with her thumb on the starter. Her foot was on the gear, ready to strike. The Kawasaki Ninja itself was pumped to take off anytime.

After a few minutes, Azra heard footsteps stomping closer. She couldn't drive off – that would be giving away her location. She must stand her ground.

She took out her gun and leveled it in the direction. The footsteps got louder and more threatening. She tightened her grip on the gun, poised and ready to pull the trigger.

But in a moment, Sylvester dashed out.

"Whoa!" he exclaimed, raising his hands in submission.

"Come on, let's get outta here." She tucked the gun back in the holster.

Sylvester got on the bike, holding onto his rifle.

"Here!" Azra gave him the bottle.

"Oh shit, you got it!" He took it from her.

The bike whirred to life. Azra revved it once and then zoomed off. The guards chased after them, firing shots, but they were far gone.

"Great job, guys," Zuri hailed.

"What about the security cameras?" Azra asked as they sped down the byway.

"I blanked them."

She was going to ask what she meant by that – but it was better when they got to the base.

She raced down the tracks like it was a competition, leaning inward at rotaries and turning in sharp bends.

The doorway soon clanked, and the Kawasaki growled in, with the bunker walls exaggerating the sound.

"Welcome back!" Zuri left her chair and stood by the analytical screen. "The time was wrong."

"No, it wasn't," Sylvester replied, coming to the screen. "Making the operation before time was their best bet at getting the target. Unfortunately for them, we were already there before the time."

He laid the bottle on the table. Azra came and stood with them.

"Erm, why is it wrapped with a cloth?" Zuri inquired.

"Disguise!" Azra answered and took the bottle.

She untied the rope around the cover, and the cloth fell loose. Her eyes were curious, and her senses were alert as she unwrapped the bottle.

It was a 1-liter bottle in the shape of a decanter. Inside it was a yellow liquid like an elixir. It had tiny bubbles that reflected the lights in the bunker.

"I wonder what project they need this for." Azra's voice came in a whisper.

Sylvester took the bottle and turned it over in his hands.

"I looked it up extensively, but nothing work taking home. These are just some physical properties the writer wasn't sure of. I think that's why it's remained classified. Neither the chemical nor the information about it is for public consumption."

It clinked as Sylvester dropped it back on the glass. "Whatever the project is, I don't think it's good."

"It isn't," Zuri agreed. "Question is: what do we do with it?"

"It'll be here until we figure out something," Azra answered rather decisively.

She took her gun to the north wall and hung it there. She glanced at the time. It was 1:55 am.

"So what do we do next?" Sylvester turned his attention to her.

Azra walked closer, staring at him in the face. "I thought you were supposed to stop after this?"

"Nah, changed my mind. It felt good being out in the field after a long time."

Zuri swiveled around. "So you're gonna continue with us?"

"Something like that." Sylvester nodded.

"Great! Welcome aboard!" Her face crinkled with a bright smile.

Having an ex-military member in their squad meant greater fighting power. At least Azra would have a partner.

With a smile on her face, she extended a hand of partnership. Sylvester locked in.

THE DETECTIVE

Azra and her squad burst an operation at Amalex Limited last night. It would seem like she had cleared her name. It would seem like she had redeemed her reputation. But that was not the case.

Protests erupted in major parts of the city in the morning. Placards hung between weary yet determined hands. One of them read:

"AZRA IS THE THIEF"

Another read:

"WE WANT AZRA ARRESTED!"

A woman held up another placard that read:

"WHY DO YOU ENJOY KILLING PEOPLE? YOU SHOULD BE A SUPERHERO, NOT A SUPER VILLAIN."

It had been reported that Azra masterminded the attack at Amalex Limited last night. She was reported to have made away with 'an essential chemical'. Although Zuri had blanked the cameras, a couple of eyes caught sight of her. And that would make the hunt for her stronger.

Jasmine had been standing in front of the TV. Now she padded to the chair and sat down – it growled and squeezed under her weight. She stared at the blank TV with her fingers interlocked beneath her jaws. She turned it off as she did not want to see more protests. But how could they forget so soon? How could they forget what she had done for the city – catching the bad guys and bursting operations? The same people singing her praise on the media were the same people calling for her arrest.

She let off some air and rubbed down on her hair. Her heart felt like it had a hundred-pound weight pushing against it. She pouted, slowly allowing more air through her lips – an exercise her therapist taught her. Therapist! Yes, therapist!

She quickly got on her feet. As she took a step toward the staircase, her phone rang on the stool next to the chair. She looked. It was Melissa's teacher. A light frown folded up her brows, but she did not answer. She stared at the phone until it stopped ringing.

Another step toward the staircase, and the phone rang again. But she merely glanced at it this time and continued on her way. She was not in the mood to answer. Whatever it was could wait. For now, all she wanted was a tablet of Pantorex.

But as night drew in, she wanted even more.

Detective Olsen alighted from the taxi and walked toward his house. It had been an exhausting day trying to uncover Azra's whereabouts. Just a tall man with a square jaw, like an ancient Egyptian model doing his job. But Azra wanted to make it easier for him.

His door and windows were just as he left them in the morning. No forced entrance. And that made him oblivious to the fact that someone had already gone through. The key snapped twice – others in the bundle jiggled.

The smell of lime wafting through his nostrils as he went through confirmed he was in the right house. He locked the door and then switched on the lights. Taking a deep breath, he took off his denim jacket and padded toward the room. But Azra's voice broke his movement:

"Detective Olsen!"

He turned sharply in the direction the voice had come, pulling his gun off its holster strapped to his waist: "Stop right there! One more move, and I'll blow your fucking head off."

Azra stood by the window, having just emerged from behind it. She was carrying the bottle of Xyline in her hand, covered with the piece of cloth

"If I wanted to harm you, I would have done that long ago…"

"Yeah. Now turn back and put your hands above your head."

Azra closed her eyes. But it was for a moment. And when she opened it, the gun flew from Olsen's hand and dropped on her hand. It was a magnetic force that he couldn't resist.

His eyes widened with terror as she held the gun up. He might look like he wasn't going to surrender, but the flush on his face betrayed him. His Adam's apple bobbed up and down as he swallowed hard. But Azra merely threw the gun on the couch a few feet away from him.

"I hope that tells you that I am not here for trouble. I just want you to listen to me."

Detective Olsen seemed a bit calm now. He stood, gazing at her, with his hands on his waist. It might look like there were no more weapons around it, but Azra was still cautious with the movement of his hands.

"What is it you want to say?" he inquired, dropping his chest with a breath.

"For more than 6 months, I have served this city. You've been a detective here throughout this time. You can affirm that. Recently, someone has been trying to ruin the good image I have built as a patriotic citizen of Wonder City. Somehow, an alter ego has risen somewhere and is determined to turn the face of this city against me. It is that person you should be looking for, not me."

"Nice try! You're tryna push your offenses on someone else – that's some lazy move."

"I am telling you the truth, Detective!"

"And you think I'm just gonna believe that? You were at the crime scenes right when the crime occurred."

Azra sighed, allowing a moment of silence. That pretty much seemed to calm the atmosphere.

"I was there to help. I got a message from Dr. Fowler, who had someone in the clinic. He told me about the abduction and the time. But by the time I got there, the abduction had been carried out. I had just disrupted a robbery at WC Bank when I discovered it was a plot to keep me busy while the main operation, which was the abduction of the two scientists, went on. Dr. Fowler was my friend. When I learned that his life was at risk, I went to save him. But the bomb had already been planted, and it was just a few seconds left. There was nothing I could do."

Detective Olsen scratched his jaw. Azra's words appeared to have triggered thoughts in his mind. "And what about the operation at Amalex Limited? There were clear indications that you weren't there to save the night."

"The same person abducted the scientists and the infants. The same person killed Dr. Fowler. The same person sent people to steal a chemical from the company. I only went there to stop the robbery. And here is the chemical they went for."

She put forth the bottle. Detective Olsen gave her an apprehensive glare. But then he summoned the courage to step forward.

"The chemical is known as Xyline," Azra added. "Little or nothing is known about it. The information is somewhat classified. But perhaps with your position, you can crack that protocol and find out more about it."

The detective turned the bottle over in his hands. A strong urge to remove the piece of cloth haunted his hands. But he thought it was better done later.

"Someone is trying to set me up, Detective…"

"And who might this be? You got any idea?"

"Not yet, but soon enough. I am not the enemy, Detective. A proper investigation will tell you that."

She walked to the door. But as she grabbed the door's handle, she looked back: "No one should know that the chemical is in your possession, Detective, until it is returned to Amalex Limited."

She opened the door and walked out. The door gently snapped shut. Whatever Detective Olsen did with the information she had just shared with him was entirely up to him. She hoped, however, that he would do the right thing.

She ghosted through the dark to the fir tree where she had parked her bike. It was an act fulfilling the resolve she had made earlier with Zuri and Sylvester. As much as she hoped it might clear her name, finding her alter ego was her top priority. And if Dr. Fowler were still alive, he would have had an idea of what the chemical was used for. He would have seen that she suddenly developed a new superpower. He had always emphasized the fact that she had yet to reach her full potential. Perhaps now was the time.

The bike lunged down the street toward the expressway. She thought how proud Dr. Fowler would have been if he was alive. She herself was still trying to comprehend how she was able to pull the bottle in mid-air and the gun from the detective's grip a while ago. Just like Dr. Fowler had always said, she needed to give herself time to discover her true potential. But behind his words, she wanted to discover herself in the line of fire. There was no denying, nonetheless, that she missed him.

She rode through the highway. But at the fourth exit, she branched off. Down an alley she went, taking different turns. She was not in the mood for some fast, furious ride that night. Taking a tighter route was a way to avoid the temptation.

But as she traveled down a street path, she saw a black Toyota SUV parked by the roadside. In front of it was a black BMW. Their color perfectly blended with the darkness - so much so her headlights seemed like some foreign body in a pool of white blood cells.

Azra stepped on her brakes, and the bike screeched to a halt. She turned off the headlights. Watching from a few yards away, she wondered what her husband was doing with her therapist. He owned the SUV, and she owned the BMW. Were they having an affair?

But she was too far from them to get an idea of what was going on.

She alighted from the bike and snuck toward the cars. Her brown costume was camouflaged with darkness, and her shoes were as though they had sound absorbers beneath them.

She got to the SUV and peeped through, ears listening out for the slightest sound. Darkness was against her at this point. She could barely see a thing in the car. But if they were in the SUV, it wouldn't be so dark, she thought – dark and quiet.

Now, she crept across the SUV toward the BMW. A few steps away, she noticed the inner light was on. Through the back windshield, she saw Michael and her therapist. They seemed to have just finished a discussion as the therapist handed him a file, and they shook hands.

As soon as he opened the door, Azra zipped across the space and hid behind a maple tree by the side, leaving no trace of her. Once again, darkness provided the perfect cover.

She poked her head out, watching as her therapist drove away. Her husband got into the car, too, with the file in his hand. His headlights soon revealed a lonely road with a trail of maple trees on both sides. Gently, he drove away in the direction the BMW went.

A cluster of thoughts filled her head as she came out of hiding. It was difficult to think they were having an affair. She had been married to Michael for 8 years now – that was after they had dated for 2 years. She could almost swear he wasn't a cheat. He could be anything but a cheat. If they weren't having an affair, what then was going on between them? What kind of business did they have?

The possible answer hung right on Azra's lips. But she was finding it difficult to ponder over it. It was difficult to think that Michael or even her therapist was working against her. It was impossible to think that they were working with the same man fighting against her. The thought of the possibility scared her.

She stood by the road, gazing down the direction they both went. Emotions were starting to cloud her features. She could almost hear her heartbeat. These were two of the people she trusted the most. It had become a case of the more she looked, the less she saw. The confusion in her head was making her brain spin.

But all of that faded at the sound of Zuri's voice:

"Azra, are you there?"

Azra sniffed hard and swished a finger across her nose. "Yeah."

But Zuri was quick to notice the quiver in her voice. "Are you okay?"

Azra coughed lightly. "Yeah, I'm fine."

Zuri wasn't convinced, for it took her some seconds before speaking again: "Please report to the base; there's something I'd like you to see."

"All right, I'm on my way."

She trudged toward her bike like a wrestler that had just been defeated.

She was still not in the mood for a windy ride tonight. She maintained the normal speed limit through the city. And soon enough, she arrived at the base in one piece.

"You don't look too good," Syl observed, "did something happen out there?"

"Nothing happened. I'm fine."

Throughout her journey down the hill, she had fought so hard to bring on a cheerful countenance. But it was more difficult than she thought. Now, she had to deal with her comrades' unsettling questions and mortifying looks.

But her answer made Zuri swallow back her question and swivel to the computer.

"What did you want to show me?" Azra asked, walking toward her and taking off her gloves.

"I think I may have uncovered the research facility." She tapped on the keys.

"What research facility are you talking about?" Azra fixed her eyes on the screen as a 3D model of a map loaded. Sylvester stood on the other side, eyes on the screen too.

"The one the babies might have been taken to."

A look of curiosity washed over Azra as she gazed at the screen as she could see through it.

"How? I don't understand."

"I have a feeling Brian is beginning to suspect I'm some sort of spy. However, I..."

"Wait! Who's Brian?" Azra's brows knitted.

"My date..."

"Oh, okay."

"I got hold of his phone last night and discovered he visited one place every day, between 8 a.m. and 4 p.m., sometimes longer. I thought it was his workplace, so I copied the coordinates. When I ran it through GPS, it brought me here." She pointed at the map that had loaded on the screen.

"Where's this place?" Azra asked.

"Not one place. You can see there are different points beeping. Now, if I..." She tapped on a couple of keys again. The map was refreshed, and name tags appeared at the points. "Here we go! These are locations within a 2km radius of this..." She pointed at a point at the center of the map.

A light frown tinted Azra's face. "But why doesn't it have a name like the others."

"Because that's exactly the point they're tryna hide. This is Stalemate Sawmill – this is St. Rita's Woods –right here is Zicom Mast, and this is the road to Greenwich Autos. So why does the center focus not have a name? Brian is a scientist. And none of these places match what he does. But since he goes to this area every day, I figured the research facility was definitely this unnamed location."

Sylvester nodded. "I think you're right. Every other location within a 2-km radius has a name except that. It's only logical to think that's where he goes."

Zuri's analysis made a lot of sense. If it was indeed the research facility they had been looking for, then she was on the verge of unraveling the mystery behind her alter ego.

"You go home while I go and check it out myself," Sylvester suggested.

"Tonight?" Azra asked, concerned, as though she wouldn't go if given the chance.

"Yes, tonight," Sylvester replied assuredly.

"I think he's right, Azra. You look tired. You should get some rest. We'll let you know how it went when we gather again."

"I am…"

"Please, Azra," Sylvester shunned the protest.

Azra swallowed back the words. Her droopy eyes and saggy face were a testament to how badly she needed to rest. She herself knew it. And it wouldn't hurt her ego if she did as they said.

"Fine!" she agreed and turned her attention to Sylvester. "You be careful out there. Remember: you're checking out the place to confirm our suspicions, not to take on the operation all by yourself."

"Sure!"

She glanced at the computer screen once again and headed off to change. Zuri and Sylvester talked more about the journey. The location was 13km away from the base, somewhere in the outskirts of the city. Sylvester would have to ride with the wind if he must get there on time.

BURNING THE CORE

Jasmine had shelved her mistrust of Michael. She had allowed his words to get through to her. She had let her suspicions of him drown in the sea of love and understanding. But after what she saw last night, that feeling sprouted again.

It was impossible not to think that there was something going on between him and her therapist. There had never been a time Michael mentioned her name as a colleague. It was much harder even to think they knew each other. Her meetings with her therapist had been a secret. She did not want Michael to think she was going insane. She did not want him to start questioning her.

But now it felt like all her secrets had been laid bare. It felt like her true identity had been thrown out to the public, and everyone now knew her as Azra. Her deepest, darkest thoughts were in the open. How could she? How could her therapist sell her secrets to the public?

Jasmine sat on her bed, wondering if she should confront her therapist. She was not going to talk to her husband about what she saw; he would deny it. But she could at least spit it on her therapist's face.

However, if she did, she would only sell them what she knew. She might deny it, too, and then they would be more cautious. It was better that she played ignorantly to learn more about what was happening. She would try to maintain a good relationship with her husband, as difficult as it would be. And perhaps it was time she paid her therapist another visit.

She usually booked an appointment with her a day before. But this time, she managed to get her down for an hour…

* * *

Azra was at the base at 10 pm – cooked mind and body. Sylvester had confirmed the location. Now, she had another opportunity to clear her name.

She had had her therapist wait for an hour and not show up. Just after she had called her, she had a change of mind. It was pointless to put words in her mouth or ask questions that would arouse suspicions.

"It's a pretty big facility," Sylvester reported as they both stood by the analytical table. "Three divisions: the outer part is the main laboratory, and the middle division is more of a Storage. It's not in line with the outer division but perpendicular to it. The last division is smaller and quite hidden. There are small pods inside. I didn't see the babies but I believe that's where they are."

"How about security?"

"There are security cameras everywhere, with at least 5 guards manning each division."

"I'll take care of the cameras," Zuri cut in.

"Of course."

"What about the scientists? Did you see Drs. Mathew and Alfred?"

"I saw a couple of scientists in the main lab – about 3 of them, 2 in the third division. Not sure which one of them you're talking about."

Azra gazed at the screen. It displayed a Rubik's cube turning on all sides. It all made sense. Perhaps if they could rescue the two scientists, they would reveal who they were working with.

"How do we get in?" she asked.

"Through the second division. It might be the same number of men guarding the divisions, but I feel it'll be easier to take out the ones around the second."

"How about the environment? Covers within the perimeter?"

"They got huge maple trees strategically grown within the area. Those could serve as covers. A couple of vehicles within the perimeter, too."

Azra held a thoughtful silence. But it was not so silent as Zuri clicked away on the keyboard.

"It's gonna be a good hit if we storm that facility tonight. They won't see us coming," Sylvester added.

"We burning it to the ground," Azra broke her silence. "That's after we rescue the babies and the scientists."

"That's more like it." Sylvester scratched his jaw. The corners of his lips stretched into a menacing smile.

"We ain't sparing anyone this time. We shoot to kill…"

Zuri stopped for a moment and looked at Azra. Not only was that order new, but the bitterness that came with it. The death of Dr. Fowler must have triggered such deep loathing.

"Let's suit up."

She marched to the wardrobe. Sylvester moved over to the arms section. With a backpack he had brought from his house, he began to load bullets and different kinds of explosives. He also added lacrimators and masks. Just enough to bring down the facility.

"Please be careful, guys. Come back in one piece," Zuri warned.

"We sure will." Sylvester shoved his arm through the backpack, steaming with confidence.

Azra already went for the bike. Michael hadn't returned home when she left. She would find out soon enough if he were working for her enemy.

Outside the bunker, the tires brushed against the leafy grounds. Azra was on the handles. It was a rough path through the woods. She was not ready for the bumps and stumbling. And so through Regent Base, it was. 13 kilometers to go. She hit the gear and tore it off.

She sought vengeance. Her brain was in circles on the memories she had with Dr. Fowler. She was the only person who took her in when everyone else abandoned her. He made her understand that her sudden powers were not a curse but could be used for the greater good. Not for once did he treat her like a lab rat, but with respect and love like he would do his daughter. Above all, he kept her powers a secret. This fight was for him.

She coasted through the highway, reaching nearly 70mph. Sylvester had to put his head on the side to stop her hair from brushing against his face. It would have been an adventurous ride if they were in a romantic relationship. Seeing she was married, it may not have crossed his mind again, but he wouldn't pass on it if given the chance.

They had followed the 442 Road, ripping past Old Glen C warehouse and heading down the outskirts. It was a lonely road—the type haunted by ghosts and demons in horror movies. It was bordered by trees and bushes, their shades thickening the darkness on the road. But the grace of the Ninja's headlamps illuminated the path, revealing the tiny insects that darted about Azra's face as she tore through the wind—some of them colliding with her.

She cut off the highway and went down a byway. There were trees along this path, but not as densely packed as along the highway. They soon rode past Stalemate Sawmill. It looked like it hadn't been operational for years. On the far left was St. Rita's woods. Azra had mummified her mind, ready for the worst tonight.

She slowed down as they approached Zicom Mast, scanning the surroundings. There was hardly any source of light here, not even from the Sawmill. The only source of light was less than a kilometer away – the research facility.

"I think we should pull over by the mast. Has a good hiding place for the bike," Sylvester suggested.

Azra did not object. He had been here before and should know better. She turned off the headlamp as the mast was barely a hundred meters away. The road was free of bumps. She still had to strain her eyes in the darkness to ride through.

The structure around Zicom Mast had an embrasure that looked somewhat like a cage. It was on the opposite side of the road. Syl directed the way.

Azra soon turned off the engine, and after they alighted, she pushed the bike into the embrasure like one driving through a garage.

"So we head down on foot." Sylvester set his hands ready on the rifle.

"Yeah." Azra adjusted her mask.

But the plan had been made. She would take off the mask before they attacked. Now, they marched down the road, their searching eyes piercing through the darkness.

"Can I ask you a question?" Sylvester broke the silence. He wanted to raise a conversation as they walked nearly 500 meters.

Azra was not in the mood. But to avoid appearing unfriendly or letting her anger steal her attention from her partner, she gave in. "Yeah, go on."

"Does your husband know about your powers?"

"No."

"You don't wanna tell him?"

"Maybe not yet."

"What if he finds out some other way, just like I did? 'Cause men, it freaked me out a little bit when I did."

"Freaked me out too when I found out."

"How did you get through it?"

Azra's silence was for a moment. She was grateful he did not continue to ask about her husband. "I got help."

"Must have been difficult to accept."

"Yeah. But Dr. Fowler made me realize it was a part of me, and there was nothing else I could do but embrace it. And I did."

"Dr. Fowler: the late scientist?"

"Yeah."

Sylvester nodded. Now he understood why Azra spoke about the operation with so much bitterness in her voice. She wanted to avenge his death.

"You said you had 2 kids."

"Yeah."

"You mind telling me about them?"

"Melissa is 7. Audrey is 5. 3rd and 1st grade, respectively."

"Are they noisy? I hear kids are pretty noisy."

Azra sighed. That would have been a giggle had anger not clouded her mind. "Sometimes. But funny enough, sometimes, too, you wish they could be a little noisy."

Sylvester chuckled. "Really? Why?"

"When they're sick. You pray they get better and return to those lively, healthy children you birthed. A child getting sick can be scary, you know."

"Yeah, I can imagine. How do you even manage to be a mum and a superhero at the same time?"

"It's hard. The mum part suffers more. I think about my kids all the time. But my commitment to the cause often gets the better of me."

"Does your husband not notice when you leave the house?"

"There he goes ago," Azra heard her mind whisper.

"He's hardly at home. He's a research scientist."

"A what?" Sylvester's eyes darted. "You sure he's not one of the scientists at that facility?"

"I don't know."

"But…"

"Look, Syl, can we talk about something else?"

Sylvester fell silent at once. The message was clear: she was in no mood to talk about her husband.

She would have defended him. If she knew her husband how she ought to, she would have had much to say about his work. She wouldn't deny the possibility of him working for her enemy. But hopefully, he wouldn't be one of the scientists at the facility.

THE FACILITY

The facility's lights reached a more than 40-meter radius, bright white lights penetrating the core of darkness. One or two trucks were parked in reserve. Azra saw the maple trees grown strategically, just like Sylvester described.

They skulked behind a dumpster about 50 meters away, studying the movements around the facility.

"You said we're approaching from the second division, yeah?" Azra asked, eyes on the facility.

"Yeah."

She glanced at him as if to be sure he was still carrying the bag. "The masks."

Sylvester unzipped the bag and removed two MIRA Safety gas masks and the lacrimators. They fixed the masks on their faces, protecting their mouths, eyes, and noses. They would now rely more on signs for communication.

Sylvester led the way this time as they stole out from the dumpster. Their feet crunched against the sand. But they tried to reduce the weight on their heels by scuttling on their toes. Syl had his rifle positioned in his left hand. He was holding a canister of teargas on the other hand. Azra still had her pistols tucked down her waist and was holding two canisters in her hands.

They crept from one tree to another, keeping their invasion a secret. The second division had a wide porch. Five guards hung around the porch—three on the outside and two standing by the door. The first division had one guard at one edge of the building and another guard on the other edge—the other three manned the door.

The heroes ghosted from one tree to another, moving only when the guards looked away, even for a second. Sylvester managed to keep up.

Now, they were behind one of the trucks, observing the guards. The doors and windows were closed. But through the glass walls on the upper half of the building, Azra could see two scientists in the first division walking from one part to another.

She signed up for Sylvester to go through the second division while she herself would go through the first. He nodded.

The maple tree standing directly in front of the porch was some distance away from them. Sylvester would have to target from behind the tree to get a better shot.

Azra was faster. She whizzed across to the truck near the first division right under the guards' noses. The next tree was like that in front of the porch. There was no way she would get to it without being spotted.

The guards themselves seemed more wary of their surroundings now. Their piercing eyes were everywhere, and the grips on their rifles had grown tighter.

But Azra was not deterred. She zipped to the tree in front of the porch. One of the men spotted her. But he wasn't sure of what he saw.

"Did you see that?" he asked his colleague, eyes wild with terror and apprehension.

"Yeah." The other guy looked around. "Who's there?"

A yell broke out from the second division. Turned out Sylvester had made a move at the same time Azra did. As the guys in the first division tried to find out what was going on, Azra launched a canister of teargas.

The smell quickly permeated the space. The gas molecules could almost be seen penetrating their eyes, ears, and noses. They held their necks as the choking molecules filtered into their mouths, choking them to death like a tight noose, suffocating their breaths. Some of them tried to cover their noses with their shirts, but it was as though they were depriving themselves of the little fresh air they got. Even their skins burnt like a gaseous acid had been sprayed on them.

And while they scrambled about in pain, the heroes opened fire. Sylvester thumped toward the porch, gunning down three of them – the other two managed to escape the bullets and ran to the back of the building, probably alerting the other five guards.

Azra was already at the door, with four of the guards lying dead around her. She turned the handle and stormed in.

Sylvester was already inside the second division. He removed the C4s and other explosives and began planting them around the division.

Azra walked through the first division. Upon hearing the gunshots, the scientists had run away. Now, she was left with racks of test tubes, microscopes, computers, large experimental tables like those of a surgeon, glass screens, pieces of equipment that resembled dialysis machines and mobile ventilators, gene splicers and transcription, and chromosome analyzers, amongst others. There were also pods the shape and size of an infant coffin connected to vats through rubber pipes of wide diameter.

Just as she skipped toward the door that led to the second division, two guards stormed through the entrance. They shot at her, but she dove behind the vat next to her. Another bullet tore through the vat, shattering it and spilling a mass of green, slimy liquid on the floor.

Azra dashed behind a mobile ventilator and fired shots at the men. They quickly took cover behind a silver table.

Sylvester opened the door, separating the first division and the second. But a horde of bullets came at him. He was fast enough to shut the door. The bullets spattered on it. However, he had already spotted Azra's position.

Azra shot at the men, keeping them down. Sylvester seized the opportunity and opened the door. He threw the backpack at Azra and shut the door again. She knew what it was for.

She picked up the bag and broke her cover, shooting at the men all the while. She had removed her mask at this time.

But not long enough, her gun went blank. The men quickly noticed and got back up. She raised her hands in submission. They leveled their guns at her, not firing immediately. Big mistake!

She shut her eyes. And in a moment, the guns snapped out of the men's grip and dropped on her hands. Two shots, and they both dropped on the floor.

"I NEED COVER!"

That was Sylvester's voice, sounding distant. She surmised it was definitely from the third division. Now, she needed her speed more than ever.

Perhaps her muscles were fired up because she was agitated and acting under tension. In less than a minute, she had planted a couple of explosives around the walls of the first division, whooshing from one end to another as swift as the wind.

With the men's guns in her hands and the backpack hanging down her shoulder, she stormed through the door. There were more cartons here and several pieces of equipment. Sylvester had laced everywhere with explosives already.

She navigated her way toward the door leading to the third division. But some men charged out from their hiding places as though they had been waiting for her and opened fire. She took cover behind a machine. Bullets clattered on the steel parts of the machine. But she couldn't continue to exchange bullets here. For Sylvester to have called for backup meant he was onto something.

She stayed calm for a moment to calculate her escape route. Three rows of cartons stacked high were in her path to the door. And by the door was another machine in the form of that for dialysis. It would block off the bullets if she could get to it, giving her a chance through the door.

But it was still risky, even if she tried to hold the men down. She had no exact idea where or how many they were. It was a gamble.

Her chest pumped and deflated. "You can do this," she muttered to herself.

Clutching tight to her guns, she stormed out, shooting rather sporadically while her limbs carried her frame across the rows of cartons. A bullet whizzed from the far right. Luckily, she saw it just in the nick of time and dived to the back of the machine by the door. Unfortunately, she landed on her elbow. A groan escaped her. Bullets tore through the machine, shattering the glasses and the plastic parts. But Azra managed to get her hands on the door, opened it, and stumbled through.

THE FACILITY II

Azra entered the third division, wincing as she kneaded her right elbow. It felt colder here. But before she could take it all in, Sylvester's voice broke in:

"We gotta get the truck fast."

Azra looked down. Three pods lay on the floor, disconnected from a vat, and other machines are sitting at a corner of the division. Through the glass, she could see the babies soaked in a green, slimy liquid, with tubes through their mouths. They looked like they were in stasis.

"Come on, each one of you carry a pod," Sylvester ordered.

Azra looked at a corner of the division and saw Drs. Mathew and Alfred cringing. They looked traumatized.

"COME ON!" Sylvester barked again.

They both shuffled closer. And while they bent over to carry the pods, Azra turned to Sylvester:

"The bombs are gonna explode any moment. We need to get out of here."

She spoke at the top of her voice as gunshots ripped through the air in different directions.

"Yeah, we need the truck to move these pods and these men."

Azra looked around. Anxiety heightened. One mistake and all that they worked for could be destroyed. The bombs were nearing zero seconds. She had jammed the door between the third and second divisions. And was it not for its extra strength, the men would have penetrated it. Now, they riddled it with bullets, slamming metal objects on it in a bid to open it. The entrance was also locked. Behind it were men trying to get through. To get to the truck, she would have to fight her way through them. At this point, only her swift movements would save them.

She looked across the upper part of the walls, searching for the main switch. But it was nowhere in this division. That, however, gave her an idea.

"All right, wait for me."

She reached for the door. At this time, the men outside had stopped shooting. They were obviously waiting for someone to come through the door.

"Careful!" Sylvester warned as he stepped away from the door and the scientists carrying the pods.

With her fingers on the handle, she took another relaxing breath. It was now or never.

She opened the door and slammed it shut. The men opened fire at once. But even before they pulled their triggers, she ripped through them to the back of the SUV a few feet away. She had managed to dodge a bullet that had almost torn through her lower abdomen.

From this spot, she took the men down one by one. She was a lost faster. The men had no chance.

And as she advanced toward the truck, the men in the second division charged out. They shot at her. But she targeted the bulb overhead and fired a shot at it. The glasses shattered into smithereens.

As the men groped about in the dark, she moved in as swiftly as a bullet. One by one, she took them out. Now, she zipped back to the truck. She opened it and stumbled in.

Her hands waved frantically as she looked for the ignition. She knew where to find it, but she was too unsettled.

"Calm down, Azra. Calm down," she whispered to herself, swallowing mouthfuls of air.

Another deep breath, and she looked behind the steering wheel. There it was – the ignition, but not the key.

"You can do this. You can do this!"

And yes, she had manipulated a car's ignition before. She looked under the wheel's bar. Luckily, it was open, and the wires were visible. She took hold of them and tore them in two. Now, she squeezed out another band of wires from farther inside. Holding them all together, she touched the tips of different colors. It was more of a try-your-luck situation in this case.

Whatever!

It worked. The truck's engine shot to life. Azra revved it again and again and then drove it closer to the third division, with the truck jerking back and forth.

"COME ON!" she yelled.

There were no gunshots to muffle the sound of her voice. She appeared to have taken out all the men. At this point, it was not about the men but the bombs.

Sylvester heard her, and in a moment, the door snapped open. He shuffled out with the scientists, each carrying the pods. Azra left the engine on and got out of the truck.

She helped with the back doors. The scientists shuffled in. There was nothing to sit on, so they would have to make do with the floor.

"Can you drive this?" she asked Sylvester, who was putting the pod in the truck and closing the door.

"Yes."

She gave way and went on to the passenger's seat. Sylvester got into the driver's seat.

"What's that?" he observed.

"What?"

He gestured at the side mirror. Azra looked into that on her side. A beam of light flashed in the distance like it was coming closer.

"I think they called for backup. Come on!"

Sylvester revved the truck and turned the steering. He reversed frenziedly and headed toward the exit. They both jerked back and forth as the truck thundered on. Putting on their seatbelts was imperative at this point. But that would stifle Azra's movements if they must fight the men speeding toward them.

The truck had only gone a few yards when the facility exploded. Objects flew in the air amidst the inferno and a thick cloud of smoke. As the explosions rocked more parts of the facility, waves transmitted across the ground vibrated the truck's tires. It skidded and swayed sideways. Sylvester held on to the steering, trying to achieve better control and balance of the tires.

But as the truck went farther from the explosions, it regained balance.

"I'm taking the road to Greenwich Autos."

Azra did not object. She knew it was a way to avoid crossing paths with the approaching men. The problem was how to get back the Kawasaki Ninja.

"Hold on, Syl," Azra broke off. "I think I should go get the bike. You continue on this way. We'll meet at Landon's Square."

"You sure about that?"

"Yeah."

"Landon's Square is less than a mile from the facility," Zuri threw in.

Sylvester slammed on the brakes, and the truck juddered to a halt.

"I'll be waiting for you at the rendezvous. Drive safely." Azra got out of the truck and slammed the door shut.

Sylvester pulled on the gear lever and fired the truck. It growled on.

Azra looked the other way. The backup had just arrived at the facility. With the blazing inferno reaching the skies, she could see them looking around. She thought they might decide to track the truck and go after it. Distracting them would be a good idea.

She ran toward Zicom Mast for her bike. Her elbow still hurt, but not so bad she couldn't handle a gun.

A second thought waltzed into her mind while she ran: since the backup saw neither her nor the truck, it was best to leave it that way. It was pointless steering up their trouble by trying to distract them.

When she got to her bike, the men were still hanging around the burning facility. Darkness thickened as the night deepened, and a warm atmosphere hovered around the facility and across a 200-meter radius.

Azra mounted her bike and powered it on. The headlamp had been off. And in the thick darkness, she maneuvered her way out of the area.

Having traveled more than 2 kilometers, she turned on the lights and fired the bike toward Landon's Square.

Meanwhile, Sylvester was on a peaceful ride to the rendezvous. He was driving at top speed to meet Azra and talk with Zuri at the same time.

"Ever been on a ride with Azra?" he asked her.

"Of course…"

"You can pretty much guess why I'm speeding then."

"Yeah. But you gotta be careful - you have babies in your trunk."

"I'm being careful."

"Where are you at, Syl?" Azra cut in.

"About a hundred meters from Landon."

"I'm almost there."

"Guess you heard that, Juli."

She laughed softly. "Azra flies on a bike."

"Juli…"

"Yeah?"

"Patch me up with Detective Olsen."

"On it…"

The truck soon began to screech. Sylvester had reached the rendezvous. Azra was less than a hundred meters away.

"He's on," Zuri reported.

"Detective Olsen?"

"Yes, Detective Olsen on the line. How may I help you?"

"A truck awaits you at Love Garden. I'd like you and your men to go and get it."

"A truck? Hold up, who's this?"

"Azra."

Tires screeched against the ground as she pulled up at the rendezvous.

"What's in the truck?"

"Drs. Mathew and Alfred and the babies that were stolen at New Haven Clinic. You should also call an ambulance."

"Love Garden, you said?"

"Yes. And detective?"

"Yeah?"

"Be quick. Not sure how much longer the babies have."

"Right!"

A beep ended the call.

"Too slow?" Sylvester teased, looking down from the window.

"Not really. To Love Garden, shall we?"

"Of course!"

"After you…"

Love Garden was less than a kilometer from Landon's Square. The truck would get there before the police. Sylvester drove at top speed. Azra followed closely behind.

As they parked the truck in a safe space and zoomed off, sirens broke the night from a distance. Sylvester rode the bike this time. And into the galaxies, he sped.

"Welcome back, guys." Zuri swiveled around and got off the chair.

The guns clattered on the analytical table. Azra propped herself up on her hands, taking calm, deep breaths. She had taken off her mask, revealing the beauty behind it.

"There were other scientists in the facility, right?" she asked.

"Yes, 3 of them," Sylvester answered, taking off his gloves. "But the men helped them escape before I got in."

Azra had feared she might find Michael in the lab. Now she wasn't sure whether to be grateful she didn't or not.

"I'm sorry, Azra, but something happened while you were at the facility."

She looked up at Zuri. Relief drained out of her face, replaced by tension and curiosity. "What happened?"

"Dr. Kyle is dead."

"What?" her brows drew together. "Dr. Fowler's assistant?"

Zuri nodded with a solemn countenance. "I'm sorry," she added.

Azra swished her hand across her nose and dropped it on her waist, staring into the vacancy. The hinge of her jaws glided beneath her skin as she gnashed her teeth.

"How did he die?" she inquired, sniffing.

"Someone shot him in his house. I have the footage if you'd like to see it."

"Yeah."

Zuri moved over to the computer. Azra and Sylvester followed her.

She tapped on a couple of keys and rolled the mouse. The footage came on screen. It showed Kyle sitting on the chair and a hand pointing a gun at him. The camera revealed the hand from the elbow.

Kyle appeared to have glanced at the person. And just as he looked away, they pulled the trigger. The bullet tore through his temple as he dropped on the couch on his side. And then the hand withdrew from the camera.

The video was not on repeat. When it ended, it returned to where the hand was pointing the gun at Kyle. Zuri gazed at the screen. She could tell why he was killed. He kept his promise to Dr. Fowler. He took her secret to his grave.

Thoughts meant to bring a tear to her eye flooded her mind. But she was distracted by something in the video.

"Can you zoom in on the hand?"

Zuri took the mouse and brought the image closer to the screen. Azra's eyes widened as she tried to take in as much detail as possible from the unclear video. Zuri zoomed further in.

"Stop!"

She squinted as she brought her eyes closer to the screen. She took over the mouse and zoomed further in on the hand. Now, her eyes settled on what looked like a tattoo drawn between the thumb and the index.

She zoomed in again on the image of a butterfly. Recognition dawned on her. She withdrew from the computer but still gazed at it.

"You know who it is?" Sylvester asked.

Azra nodded. She had gone white in the face.

"Who?"

"My friend, Susan. She's had that tattoo for as long as I can remember."

Silence simmered. Everyone took a moment to digest what had just been revealed.

Zuri took a closer look at the image. "Why did your friend have to kill Dr. Fowler's assistant? Do you think she might be working for the enemy?"

"It's possible. And I think she killed him because he probably refused to disclose my true identity."

"I don't think that's why, " Sylvester said. Azra looked at him. "I have a feeling the enemy already knows who you are behind the mask. And my instincts tell me it's someone close to you."

"Yeah, I think so too," Zuri supported. "I mean, how come they know everyone that holds your secret?"

Sylvester raised a brow lightly and leaned against the control table.

"So, what do you think could be the reason behind it?" Zuri directed the question at Sylvester. Azra glanced at her.

"I don't know," he answered. "But I think there's more to this than we know..."

Words that triggered thoughts had been spoken. And these words carry a pinch of truth with them. There could indeed be more to everything than Azra knew. It could be more than her alter ego trying to bring her down. Even heavier was the speculation that her enemy could be someone close to her. Her husband, Michael, her therapist, and now her friend, Susan – the people she trusted.

MIND GAMES

Jasmine was still trying to absorb the fact that the people she trusted had betrayed her. One of them was her enemy. And on the one that pulled a trigger lay the greater suspicion.

She would never have believed Susan could hurt a fly had she not seen it herself. It was unbelievable how people could change over a few years, how the man she knew and loved turned into a total stranger.

After the kids had gone to school, she had turned the bedroom she shared with Michael upside down. She was looking for a clue—a clue to his involvement with all that had been happening to her. From the closet, his clothes, to the drawers, even to the floorboards, she found nothing worth pondering. He was careful not to let any sensitive information lie around, not after what happened the last time his wife saw what was written on that piece of paper.

She was exhausted after a long search. She dropped on the bed, refilling her lungs with fresh air from whence she dozed off.

She woke up at around 1:30 p.m. Sitting on the bed, she rubbed her hands on her face and yawned deeply. The room was a mess—clothes and papers littered everywhere. But time was not on her side. She had to clean and go pick her kids up from school.

She stood up from the bed and stretched. Her mouth broke open with a yawn. And as she let the air out, her phone rang.

She shuffled to the table. An unknown number was calling. Her eyes shifted back and forth as she wondered who it could be.

She slid her index finger across the phone and put the call on speaker.

"I must commend your bravery last night. You know, it still surprises me how you got to find out about the research facility. I must say I am impressed. You rescued the babies and the scientists – something the police could never have been able to do…"

"Who are you?" Jasmine inquired – her eyes burnt with anger and curiosity.

"I think you should be more concerned about your kids at this point."

Jasmine's eyes lit up. "What are you talking about? What have you done with my kids?"

"Uh, I gotta be honest with you: your kids aren't safe where they are. But I promise that if you follow my instructions, you'll find out where they are…"

"I will kill you. I will destroy…"

"Yes, yes, you'll do all that to me. But I advise you to shut up and listen to me. Your children have C4 bombs on them. It is not a timer. You need a detonator to cause an explosion. The detonator is under a thin hydraulic pump. And as we speak, the pump is pushing down toward it. You will need a key to stop the pump…"

"And you think I'm going to fall for this trap? Think again, you faceless coward!" Jasmine's cheeks had turned crimson.

"You must be dumb to think that I'll waste my time on things that do not matter. I dare you to call my bluff and watch your kids blow up in small chunks. I'll be sure to send you the video."

Jasmine took a breather and swallowed hard. It was a risk she couldn't take. "Where can I find this key?" she asked.

"On the fifth floor of Swiss 40."

"What?"

"You have 5 minutes to get the key. If you do, I'll tell you where the detonator is. You know what will happen if you don't."

The call ended with a beep. Jasmine looked around the room as if forgetting something. Delay could be dangerous. She snatched her phone from the table and dashed out of her room.

On her way out of the house, she texted Zuri:

"Someone has my kids. There's a bomb on them. I'm on my way now to get some keys like he instructed. I need you to tap into my phone conversations with him. He said he would call again. And stay on the line."

Anxiety clutched on her muscles. She ran as frantically as a mother whose newborn had been stolen. She was certain she would rescue her children. And when she did, their teachers would explain to her how someone managed to abduct them from the school before the closing time.

She scurried out of an alleyway. And just then, a dispatch rider came along. She waved rather recklessly at him. Immediately he pulled over, she took hold of the handle:

"Police: I need your bike."

She pushed him off the bike, mounted it and zoomed off. The man could only give a distant call.

Swiss 40 was about two miles away. Although the bike she snatched may not be as fast as her Kawasaki Ninja, it could still get her to the place in time.

Speed limits along the road didn't matter at this point. She could care less about the police, too. She cruised at top speed like she did at night, swaying past cars and other bikes as if they were in slow motion.

Swiss 40 was somewhere beyond the city's commercial area. It was an office building razed by fire about a year ago and had been abandoned ever since. Jasmine pulled over and laid the bike on the ground. Her lissome limbs took her swiftly into the building.

Debris from the fire littered everywhere—woods, papers, and all. Even after a long time, it still smelt of burns. Jasmine located the staircase on her right. Since no one was in here, she applied her supernatural speed.

The 5th floor was not easy to reach through the staircase. It would take her several minutes to get there. She hadn't checked the time since she started her journey, but she believed she was probably a minute before the time.

She ripped through the staircase, navigating the curves as required. It was exhausting, like some hurdle race. From the first floor to the fifth floor, it took less than a minute.

She arrived at a wide-open space. Chairs and tables were burnt beyond repair and scattered everywhere. Ash, steel rods, and papers that had escaped the fire were on the floor. Jasmine looked around, not sure where to find the key.

She finally tapped on her phone. It had been exactly five minutes since the call ended. He would call at any moment.

And as she raised her eyes from the phone, they fell on a plank lying flat on the floor. On it was a single key. In a blink of an eye, Jasmine reached for it.

Immediately she picked it up, her phone gave off life. It was the unknown caller. Like before, she put the call on speaker.

"My mother would take the greatest risk to save me, too. My sister killed my father a few years ago. The same man my mother loved so much. But she thought he was stupid to have married her mother. And…"

"Can you stop this bullshit and tell me where to find my kids? I don't care about your story…"

"You will when the time comes. Okay, so you found the key. Now, let's take you to the detonator, shall we? I'd like to know where the most likely places hydraulic pumps should be found are."

Jasmine wheeled her eyes round their sockets. She knew the answer, but the anger in her wouldn't let her think. "I don't know."

"Oh, disappointing! Come on, Jasmine, think!"

Jasmine swallowed a lump of saliva and a breath. "Construction or automobile companies."

"That's close enough! The detonator is at Auto Crush, behind the spot that mirrors the sun at noon…"

"I don't under…"

"You will not be timed as the pump is already a few centimeters away from the detonator. Your kids' lives are in your hands."

The call ended once again with a beep.

Jasmine had no idea where to find Auto Crush, but maybe the internet would give her an idea. She used her phone to access Google Maps.

Auto Crush was 4km from Swiss 40, less than 200 meters from Old Glen C warehouse.

As if blown by the wind, she whooshed down the staircase. Her supernatural speed would have been most helpful at this time. But she wasn't sure she could run 4km.

She mounted the bike again and rode off. Luckily, the police hadn't surrendered the building yet after she had broken many traffic rules on her way there.

There were more traffic rules to break as she coasted down the highway at top speed. The bike was pretty light to handle and flowed well in the direction of the wind.

Using Old Glen C as a focal point, she soon arrived at Auto Crush, a car–crushing site. Car doors, bumpers, windshields, and other car parts were littered everywhere. On the left was a pile of cars that had been crushed somewhat like a dumpsite. On the right was the machine responsible for the demolitions—the crusher.

Jasmine was lost. Where could she possibly look? But the man's words soon flitted into her head: "Behind the spot that mirrors the sun at noon." The words echoed in her head again and again. And as it did, she looked around.

She gazed skyward. It was long past noon, and the sun was on its way down the west. Noon was midday, exactly 12.00 pm. At this time, the sun should be in the middle of the sky.

Still gazing up at the sky, she moved to the left and to the right, back and forth, trying to pick the most probable point.

One more step to the right, her temple knocked against a steel pipe jutting out from a heap of scraps. She yelped and rubbed on the spot. The pipe had broken her skin. She was bleeding.

But as she looked down, she saw the pump—a small pump as thin as the man had described. It was less than an inch close to the detonator, which looked so much like a car remote. Jasmine bent and snatched the detonator at once.

She gazed intently at it, turning it over in her hand while taking deep breaths. She looked at the pump. It was pressing against the steel cylinder. And Jasmine's phone chimed again:

"Nothing beats the determination of a mother to save her child, my mum will always say. Not sure the same could be said about your own mother, Jasmine."

"Speak about my mother in that manner again, and I will find you and cut your body into tiny pieces and feed them to the vultures…"

"There is no need for threats, my dear. I can assure you that the end is near. Now, let's reunite a mother and her kids. So… where are they? Hmm… yeah, Witch's Lair. That's where they are."

"What? Do you dare set my children up in such a bizarre place? I swear to God, I will find you. And when I do, you'll regret ever being born."

"Easy with the threats, Jasmine. You ain't gon' do shit. And do not think you alone have the detonator. I have it here, too. If you have more threats, I'll press just one button. So shut the fuck and go get your kids."

The phone beeped. With taut facial muscles, Jasmine bit hard on her lower lip and clenched her teeth. If the phone had not been strong enough, she would have crushed it as she gripped it too tight, like she was in a tug-of-war.

She stormed toward the bike, thinking about Witch's Lair. She had only been there once - some abandoned area in the far east of Wonder City.

She would have called for backup, but she didn't think the man would be at the location. Even if he was, she was convinced she could handle him alone. All that mattered was getting her kids to safety.

WITCH'S LAIR

Jasmine traveled 7km toward the outskirts of the city. The sun scorched her skin even as she cut through the warm air. She was putting on a black jeans trouser and a sleeveless top. The parts of her that were not covered were tanning. The wind blew against her hair – strands of it matted on her face as she journeyed on. Her hands gripped firmly on the handle, firing the bike and tooting the horn.

She was not on a countdown this time. And although she rode at top speed, she was more conscious of the road than before.

She veered down the byway that led to the location. It was not tarred and had dry bushes on both sides. The bushes were not so thick, so she could see through the spaces. There were not so many trees here, and it was windy. Jasmine had slowed down, but her hair still frizzled in the wind.

Witch's Lair was a bungalow, standing alone in an expanse of an almost-barren space. About 20 meters from it was a 90's Mercedes clothed with dust, making it almost unrecognizable. Another structure that looked like a security tower in a military base stood at the far side of the building. Woods scattered here and there. Jasmine would have come with her glasses. She was on some casual visit, for it rained dust here. The atmosphere was made slightly foggy by clouds of dust.

She stood the bike in front of the bungalow and hurried to the door. It rained dust as she put her hand on the handle, just like the walls and every other part of the building.

She opened the door and stormed inside. It slammed shut behind her. Her eyes scanned everywhere, from the shelf as big as a wardrobe to the hourglass on a table by the side to the translucent windows and vintage carvings on the roof. It looked more like a haunted house.

The open space that was supposed to be the living room had a steel chair at the center. Jasmine looked from it to the pillars some distance away and then to the staircase.

"Hello!" she called. "Is someone here?"

She walked toward the chair but quickly changed course. Now, she headed toward the staircase. But out of nowhere, something smote her head. It was like she had just been hit by a 300-pound weight. She faded instantly.

* * *

It came again in quick flashes. The voices, the buzzing of electricity, the screams, and then it all faded.

"Keep fighting, Child. You can get through this. It's not yet time to go to the other side. There's still a lot to accomplish on this side. So, fight it. Fight it, kid. And I'll be waiting for you on this side of life."

Jasmine heard this voice in her dream, calling her back to life. She could hear beeps amidst the sound of the voice. Those words armed her with the strength she needed to fight death.

And then she felt her finger move. It moved again. She could feel life returning to her limbs and other parts of her body. She heard a shuffle and the door creaking.

Slowly, she opened her eyes. It was blurry at first, but her eyes soon got acquainted with the white roof overhead. It dazzled her eyes a bit. And then she looked into the thin grey light of the room – a hospital room. She had an oxygen mask on her nose. An ECG stood next to her gurney – the source of the beeps.

While she took in the features of her environment, the door snapped open. A doctor, two nurses, and a man in a two-piece suit walked through.

"What a miracle!" he exclaimed.

The doctor moved over and placed the bell of his stethoscope on her chest. He checked her wrist and her eyes. And carefully, he removed the oxygen mask. Again, he checked her heartbeat.

He withdrew from her while the nurses wrapped up the mask.

"Good to have you back, Miss Jasmine," he commented. He looked at the man sitting beside the gurney. "We'll be back to run further tests and evaluations."

"Okay. Thank you."

The doctor and nurses left the room. She looked at the man, wondering why the medics would trust him enough to leave her alone with him. She had not met him before.

"With the look on your face, I know you're wondering who I am." He had a small smile on his face as he spoke. "My name is Dr. Fowler Augustine. I've been visiting ever since you were brought in. And I'm standing in as your guardian."

"What?" She tried to get up but felt pain ripple through her head and down her spine. She groaned, breathing through clenched teeth.

Dr. Fowler had moved in and tried to put her back on the bed. "Lie still. You're not strong enough."

"Don't touch me!" she spat, retracting her body from his.

"I understand how you feel, and believe me, I mean you no harm. You have great potential, and I can help you." He got on his feet and adjusted his suit and glasses. His paunchy belly came first. "I'll be back when you're in a better mood. And by the way, I'm sorry about your parents."

He pulled on his suit and walked toward the door. But Jasmine stopped him:

"Wait!"

He turned and then walked back to the bed. The words were at the tip of her tongue but difficult to say. Dr. Fowler stayed quiet, allowing her to fight her reluctance.

"My parents: where are they?" Her voice broke almost in a whisper.

"I'm sorry, but their bodies have been deposited in the morgue."

Jasmine was quiet. A cloud of grief had begun to gather overhead. She sniffed hard and asked: "what about my brother?"

Dr. Fowler clicked his tongue. He made a scene while you were being loaded into the ambulance. 'Cause of that, the hospital management restricted him from seeing you for the reason that he was potentially dangerous. But I guess we don't all handle the death of our loved ones the same way, do we?"

That cloud of grief broke over Jasmine, and out came the tears. They rolled down the corners of both eyes.

"I'm sorry, my dear." He went and sat on the bed. He took hold of her hand and massaged it tenderly. "You're not alone, Child. I'll be here whenever you need me. I'll help you get through this phase, okay…?"

"Wake up, shawty. Wake the fuck up! Are you still out? Come on! Wake the fuck up!"

This deep, distorted voice continued to yell in the background. It was like that of a robot or some horrifying demon. It echoed louder, masking Dr. Fowler's voice until Jasmine could no longer hear it.

She jerked and shook her head. She opened her eyes slowly. Water dripped all over her body like she was just coming out of a pool. Gradually, everything came to focus.

"Crazy to have kept everyone waiting," a voice broke the silence.

Jasmine looked up. Her face went pale in an instant at what she saw. Her brother, Clark, her therapist, Dr. Krishna, and her friend, Susan, stood before her. On both sides were 5 men – some of whom had guns with them.

"I didn't think it would take almighty Azra a splash of water to recover from a minor blow."

"What is going on, Clark? Dr. Krishna? Susan?"

She tried to get up. But she could not. The legs of the chair scraped on the ground. She looked and realized she was chained to the chair. "Clark? You've been the enemy all along?"

"I am much worse than that. I recruited everyone close to you, including your husband – all for one reason…"

"Which is?"

"To kill you slowly. Don't think about it; we all share the same cause – they all want you dead, too. But guess what? There's a greater cause. My mother loved that stupid father of ours so much that she sacrificed everything for him – her pride as a woman, her money, and even her own family. But he dumped her and married your mother…"

"Wait, so this is all about revenge!"

"It is much more than that. But isn't it worth every blood?" He walked closer, rhythmically knocking the heels of his shoes and his walking stick. My mother made your father who he was. But he abandoned her for your mother because 'he was at peace with her.' Really?" He went behind the chair and rested his hands on her shoulders. "What he didn't know was that she was pregnant with me. But you know…" he came and stood before her again, "even after everything he did, my mother still loved him. All he needed to do was apologize, and she would run back into his arms. But although he did nothing like that, she still foolishly loved him. Now imagine how she felt when she learned that his daughter from the woman she hated most killed him?"

"It was an accident!"

"IT WAS NEVER AN ACCIDENT! YOU CREATED THAT SHITTY MACHINE JUST TO KILL HIM."

"But I lost my mother too."

Clark recoiled, having just yelled at the top of his voice. Jasmine always got emotional whenever she was guilt-tripped. Her voice quivered as she replied to him remorsefully.

"Your mother's death was only collateral damage. But trust me, if she hadn't died, we would have killed her. I was never in that house as a family. My mum agreed that I come live with you so I can gather all the necessary information to nail your mother."

"What?" the corners of Jasmine's eyes crinkled.

"Yes. And if I had the chance, I would have killed you in that hospital. Well…" he stretched out his hands, "I'm glad I didn't…" he backed away from her and took his place between the two women. "How could I have known that I could become a god amongst men and rule the world? My mother had her men keep a close watch on you. And then they discovered that you had developed some superpowers due to the electrical discharge that day. My mother thought those powers befit an alpha male like me more than a lowlife. All that plotting has led us to where we are now."

Jasmine listened as her brother, whom she trusted so much, said these vile things to her. She gazed at him through a mist of tears. To think that he was the only person in the world she trusted even more than herself made it more heartbreaking. It dawned on her once again how much Dr. Fowler had meant to her.

"And Dr. Fowler? Did you have to kill him? What about his assistant, Dr. Kyle? Did you have to kill him too?" She looked at Susan – a tear rolled down her cheek. "Did you have to kill him?"

Susan looked like she still had her humanity. She refused to make eye contact with Jasmine and faced the floor.

"They were two of the brightest scientists in the state, especially Dr. Fowler. Having learned that they both helped you through your self-discovery stage, we thought they could greatly help us. With a sample of your blood, which your husband provided, and the stem cells from the babies, we thought we could create even greater superpowers. But those fools refused to work with us. We had no choice but to eliminate them. But we went ahead with the project, regardless. It was a work in progress until you ruined everything by blowing up the facility. But I assure you, we ain't gonna quit. We'll try again and again and again."

Jasmine sniffed hard. Tears welled up in her bloodshot eyes. But they dropped off at the corners when she looked up at Clark: "So all this is just to acquire superpowers?"

"You must understand that the mission is not centered on one goal. That is why we will not hesitate to take out anyone that stands in our way, including you, my lovely sister."

Jasmine swallowed back what was left of her tears and sniffed. "Where are my kids?"

"Oh, yeah, your kids are hanging down Tomlin's Tower. There are no bombs on them. All that was just to lure you here."

"You…" Jasmine tried to fight free, but the chains gripped her wrists and ankles to the chair.

"Don't worry about your kids. I'm sure the police will find a way to bring them down. I think you should be more worried about yourself 'cause you have a lot coming your way…"

Back in the heart of the city, Sylvester had just walked out of a mall. He was munching on a bar of chocolate while walking down an alley with his bags hanging down his hand. But then he heard someone call from behind:

"Hey, excuse me."

He looked back, with cheeks swollen. Michael scurried toward him. With a loose tie and shirt half-buttoned, he looked overwhelmed with anxiety.

"Yeah, how can I help you?" Sylvester asked, swallowing the last bit of chocolate in his mouth.

"My name is Michael, and I am Jasmine 's husband." His voice and even his body trembled as he spoke. Those round brown eyes had turned hazel. Now they fluttered with anxiety.

"Hold on, you're Jasmine 's husband?" Sylvester asked like he was about to land him a powerful punch if he affirmed.

"Yes. Look, I know I've not been a good husband. I've worked for the wrong people. And it wasn't my fault. They- they threatened to kill my kids if I didn't do as they asked…"

"Wait, wait, wait, slow down. Who are you talking about? Who are the people?"

"The Triagon. They're a group of powerful men and women on a very dark mission. They made me do horrible things."

"Yeah, so what do you want?"

"They have my wife and my kids. I need your help to get them back. I know you've formed some kind of team with my wife…"

"What? I don't know what you're talking about. And I can't help you."

Sylvester walked away. But Michael went after him, his knees managing to keep his feet on the ground.

"Don't walk away, please. There's nothing to hide, okay? Your name is Sylvester, a former military agent. You and Jasmine were classmates back in high school. I know all this because the Triagon has all the information about you. I am willing to work with you and give you any information you may need. Please! My family is in serious danger. Help me!"

Sylvester couldn't help but feel pity for him. He was literally shaking all over. Droplets of sweat scattered on his forehead.

"It's all right. Do you have any idea where they're being kept?

"No, I don't. But…"

Sylvester's phone rang in his pocket. He took it out. It was Zuri.

"Juli…?"

Silence.

"All right, I'm on my way." The call ended. He turned his attention to Michael. "I think we might have an idea where they are. Put in your phone number. I'll call you if we need anything from you."

"All right." Michael took the phone from him and typed in his phone number. "Thanks, man."

"I gotta go. And hey, do not get the police involved yet. We'll let you know when to do that."

"Okay."

Sylvester scurried away, heading straight to the base. Zuri would work her fingers on the keys and uncover the location where Jasmine was being kept. Sylvester was already pumped for the rescue mission. He would not go alone. Zuri was also ruggedly built for the field. They could still have Jasmine's kids if the police hadn't already, like Clark said.

For an ex-agent like Sylvester and a true crusader like Zuri, they would either save Azra or die trying. Whatever the case might be, the battle had just begun.